D1106683

I AM CANADA

Storm the Fortress

The Siege of Quebec

by Maxine Trottier

Scholastic Canada Ltd.

Toronto New York London Auckland Sydney
Mexico City New Delhi Hong Kong Buenos Aires

A Dear Canada Book. Published by Scholastic Canada Ltd.
SCHOLASTIC and I AM CANADA and logos are trademarks
and/or registered trademarks of Scholastic Inc.

www.scholastic.ca

Library and Archives Canada Cataloguing in Publication

Trottier, Maxine
Storm the fortress : the siege of Quebec / Maxine Trottier.

(I am Canada)
ISBN 978-1-4431-0007-6

1. Québec Campaign, 1759--Juvenile fiction. I. Title.
II. Series: I am Canada

PS8589.R685S76 2013   jC813'.54   C2012-905326-0

6 5 4 3 2 1   Printed in Canada 114   13 14 15 16 17

The display type was set in Attic.

First printing January 2013

For the Anderson boys: Jacob, Luke and Will

Prologue

I raced around the deck with the other boys, pretending that we were sailors. We squinted into the sky, licking our fingers to test the direction of the wind. At six, I was as free as the fish that swam in the depths beneath the *Alderney*. It was the spring of 1750 and my family and I were sailing from our village of Brierly-by-the-Sea in England to the new settlement of Halifax in Nova Scotia. A good life awaited us. Things would be different than they had been in England. Father, who was paying for part of our passage by working as a seaman, would own land. He would be a farmer rather than a sailor, and Mother would have her own house. As for me, who could say what great deeds I would do?

My mother would laugh at all of this. How my father smiled at her happiness and our good luck.

Luck has a way of disappearing, though.

Chapter 1
1750

Storms and huge breaking waves tossed the *Alderney* around violently. Water poured down through the poorly fitting hatches and creaking deck boards. At night, the ship groaned as powerful gusts of wind roared through the rigging. The smell of vomit never left my nostrils.

When the fresh vegetables and fruit were gone, we had nothing to eat but salt beef and ship's bread. Those rock-like biscuits were filled with weevils, but we still tried to get them down. Some of us began to suffer from scurvy. Teeth loosened. Sores and wounds that had been long healed began to open and run with pus. Death became a familiar event, as did the horrible burials at sea. Before long I could recite by heart the service the captain read as the remains of some poor soul were dropped into the cold water. At a land burial, people would be weeping and sighing, but here every eye was dry. No one had tears to spare for the dead.

My mother died only a week before *Alderney* reached land. She too was buried at sea, of course.

It was impossible to bring her remains to shore. I kept dreaming of the sound her canvas-wrapped body had made as the ocean received it. My father mourned her terribly. And yet, people still said how fortunate we were, that we had made the crossing in a fairly healthy ship. I wished they could have crossed with us, just to see the truth.

Halifax, when we reached it, was a surprise. Its houses were built of simple planks. Some had several chimneys because Halifax winters were wickedly cold. My fingers and nose might fall off, I was warned. After our hardships at sea, a cold winter did not frighten me.

The town was noisy, muddy, and rougher than any I had ever seen. After the tameness of Brierly, I loved it. Not everyone agreed, however. As soon as some men had a chance, they disappeared, probably slipping away to the New England colonies, where they believed life was easier.

I could not say if it was easier, but I suspect it may have been safer compared to Halifax. There was a rough log palisade surrounding the town. In it, at the top of the hill, was Fort George, named after our king.

There were also defences on Georges Island in the town's harbour, complete with cannons. But none of that protected people from what was in the wilderness just beyond the town. There were Indians out there, tribes they called the Micmac and Maliseet. Both were allied to the French. It did not take long for stories of what happened to those caught by the French and Indians to reach my ears. What night-mares I had!

My father seemed right at home in all this, though, and if he was discouraged he did not show it. A practical man, he began the business of providing for me without my mother. The idea of farming was set aside, and he went back to sea on one of Mr. Joshua Mauger's merchant vessels. *Merry Lot,* she was called. We took cheap rooms at the widow Walker's inn, and when Father sailed out I was left behind with the widow.

It was there at Mrs. Walker's inn that I learned many useful things. She taught me to wipe tables and carry cups of her spruce beer to the patrons without spilling a drop. Best of all, she taught me to read and write.

And then there was the dog.

It appeared suddenly one day. Small, brown, and spotted with white, it had very little tail at all. Mrs. Walker tried to shoo it away with her apron, but the dog growled at her. She waved the poker and banged pots, but it had no effect at all on the dog. Sometimes it wandered away on its own and Mrs. Walker sighed with relief. But then back in it would stroll when some unsuspecting sailor opened the door. They fed it bits of meat, being careful not to lose a finger. Mrs. Walker still grumbled, but even she could see that the dog was good for business.

"It needs a name," I said one day, stroking the dog's head.

"I can think of several choice things I might call it," grumbled Mrs. Walker. "Mind your fingers, William. The creature can crack a bone with those wicked teeth."

"It's a good ratter, though," I said in the dog's defence.

"True enough," Mrs. Walker admitted.

"Name it, then," said my father, who had arrived home that morning. "It is only fair, since the dog seems to like you as much as anyone. But name it well, as well as a captain christens a ship. A good ratter can do a house proud. It needs a name that it can be proud of."

Mrs. Walker shook her head. The dog was scratching itself like mad. "Fleas," she muttered.

"Well . . . I christen thee King Louis!"

"The *French* king's name?" laughed my father.

"I cannot very well name him after own King George, can I?"

And so King Louis he became. He continued to reign over Mrs. Walker's tavern, and all of Halifax was his kingdom. Sometimes he could be seen riding along with a group of sailors who were going out to their ship. It made me wonder what such a free life would be like.

Chapter 2
June 6, 1754

My father answered that question the year I turned ten, when he said that the *Merry Lot*'s captain had need of a small boy to help on the ship's next voyage. I screamed with excitement.

"Who is being murdered in here?" asked the widow. "Shall I call the soldiers to beat off the French and Indians?" But she was smiling because she already knew my father's plan.

"I am going to sea, Mrs. Walker!" I told her. "So is King Louis. I will be a sailor like my father."

I was not much more than a passenger, though, for the dozen or so times I was on *Merry Lot*. But it did not matter. During the day, unless I had chores assigned, I had the run of the decks. In the evenings I listened to my father and the other men talk their rough sailors' talk. Such stories they told about ghost ships, and adventure and the monsters that lurked in the ocean's depths! Often I fell asleep to the sound of whales calling to each other far down in the black waters.

By this time, Mr. Mauger had built himself a

rum distillery. His vessels carried rum to soldiers and settlers alike. Father's ship always sailed up the coast to a place the French called Île Royale — the British called it Cape Breton Island. And it always stopped at their fortified town of Louisbourg there.

Our ship would anchor in deep water. Then we went ashore in its smaller boats to bring in the casks. As the sailors rowed, the harbour walls drew closer. There was the archway they called the Dauphin Gate. Dauphin was what they also called the French king's son, Father told me. There on the rise was the King's Bastion.

Once we were in, Father and the other men hauled the rum to Monsieur La Chance's tavern. The captain did business with the tavern keeper while father and the sailors sat at his tables enjoying good French food and drink. Monsieur La Chance's wife served them while her son Pierre and I made horrible faces at each other.

I had the best of it, to be sure. Pierre was a small, rather wild boy, a few years older than I. Around his neck he wore a large cross that his father had carved for him from whale bone. He had a birthmark on his right cheek, one in the shape of a small fish. It was why they called him Vairon, which means minnow. Vairon spoke a little English, and I spoke a little French taught to me by

Father. It was enough to make a good beginning.

We would race around the streets and get into as much mischief as we could in an afternoon. There were goats to be teased and horses to be petted. We begged the bakers for heels of fresh, warm bread, and then wandered around laughing at people's linen hanging to dry in the sun. If the day was warm, we went down to a nearby cove and hurled ourselves into the water. It was how I learned to swim. Vairon said that with all my splashing and struggling I looked more like I was drowning.

Often we went up to the King's Bastion where Louisbourg's governor lived. We marched around like soldiers. Even better, we played at being pirates. Capitaine Rosbif, Vairon used to call me, since Englishmen, especially English pirates, were so fond of their roast beef. With King Louis at our heels, I believed I looked the perfect image of a pirate, rather than a boy with dog hair on his shirt.

Hot and sweaty, we would sneak into the ice house for chunks of ice to cool our faces and mouths. The ice house belonged to the French king, Vairon told me. We would take some back to Vairon's house and sit in his mother's raised garden bed among the cabbages and carrots, letting it melt in our mouths. We felt like kings ourselves.

"To friendship and adventure!" we would cry. It became our motto.

To be honest, Louisbourg was a much finer place than Halifax. The houses were larger and grander, the King's Bastion a thousand times more impressive than Halifax's forts. I saw people of every colour there, even black-skinned men. English and French were spoken, but so were languages I had never heard before. It put me in mind of the Tower of Babel that I had heard about in church.

But peace is like a full belly. It does not last. And war was as sure a thing as the sun rising and setting. So when fighting here began once more between England and France in 1754, my trips to Louisbourg came to an end. Father's ship still sailed out, but to my great disappointment I no longer went with him.

"I will never see Vairon again," I grumbled.

"People have an odd way of moving in and out of a man's life," Father told me mysteriously. "Wait and see what life brings."

Knowing how I felt, though, he gave me his spyglass on which were engraved his initials, *W. J.* Now I could watch *Merry Lot* as she disappeared over the horizon. Better still, I could scan the ocean for her safe return. I treasured that glass, and it was a great comfort as I wandered the town.

When Father was home we often spoke in French. A man who speaks more than one language has an advantage in this world, he insisted. But once the Acadians were rounded up and shipped off into exile in 1755, it did not seem a wise thing to do. Those Acadians were loyal to France, after all. Now and again at Mrs. Walker's, men would glance at Father and me and mumble something about smuggling — even treason — so we spoke French only when we were by ourselves, from that time on.

"Never follow a mob," Father advised me. "Remember your friends, make your own choices, and do not judge other men." I would nod at him. "And practise your letters. That is the way to success."

I was not so sure about that, but I did practise all of it. And I tried to remember my friend Vairon, but over the next few years the memories of him slipped away as surely as water through my fingers. Then he was gone.

Chapter 3
April 16, 1759

The evening began just as any evening at Walker's Inn ever did. I was my own man now at the age of fourteen, with my own friends. There I sat with my companion Baldish Sykes at our usual table near the hearth. Cups of Mrs. Walker's terrible spruce beer were in front of us.

Like many British sailors, Baldish had spent the winter in town rather than on his ship. This would be his last night ashore, since the navy was getting ready to return to war with the French.

I accepted that the French were our enemies. Surely their navy and army were. Only to myself, though, did I think that I had no argument with them. In fact, I had felt pity for the Acadians, poor miserable souls who had been deported from Nova Scotia. They had been farmers, not soldiers. Had Vairon and his parents been among those unfortunates?

"No more going out in that miserable ferry to deliver newspapers to Mr. Cook. No more Halifax snow!" Baldish cried. "No more days of rest here on shore. Ah, well. It had to end. All good things do." He winked and shouted, "To Mrs. Walker and her excellent tavern. And to the wretched French. May they sail like landlubbers and fight like parsons!" Then he whispered, "I cannot toast this beer, though. You realize what it tastes like? Piss!" He made a face.

Someone was playing a fiddle, and King Louis began howling madly, probably as an accompaniment to the song. I might have howled myself, except I was trying to listen to Baldish. It seemed that he had news of great interest.

"Did you hear about the schooner *Apollo* that came in this morning from Marblehead?" he began.

"Yes — the one from the colony of Massachusetts."

"Those Yankee volunteers she carried up?" he went on. "Well, some went aboard *Squirrel*. And seventeen of them are now on my own *Pembroke*."

From the way he always spoke, it sounded as though Baldish owned *Pembroke*. He was that proud of her. But she was one of the navy vessels, and so she was King George's.

"Well, that is a good thing, is it not? You tell me the ships are short-handed," I said, ducking to avoid an apple core someone had flung at the dog.

"Maybe yes, and maybe no. I have not set eyes on them, but I will tomorrow. I hear that Yankees can be — "

It was a cup that flew past my nose this time, hitting its mark. King Louis yelped and bolted from the room. I wiped beer suds from my cheek.

"A man who will hurt a helpless animal is a coward," I called out. I felt quite proud of myself until the thrower of the cup rose to his feet. He was a sour-faced man with bloodshot eyes. I felt certain that the days of having all my teeth in my head were over.

The man staggered over to me. "Coward, says you!" he roared in my face. His breath was as foul smelling as his greasy shirt and breeches. "No one calls Boston Ben Fence a coward and lives to say it again."

"My mistake, Mr. Fence," I apologized. The man grinned at his friends, quite pleased with himself. "I meant to call you a bully."

I barely saw his fist before it met my nose. Sprawled face down on the floor of the tavern, I noticed my blood mixing with the dirt. I was dragged to my feet. Clenching my fists, I prepared to defend myself, but it was not the bully who held me by my collar.

"That would be enough, Ben."

The speaker was an enormous fellow. From his accent, he too was a Boston man and so a Yankee, but a very strange one. His hair was a coppery red and he had the whitest skin I have ever seen. His face and arms were marked with blue designs which clearly would never wash off. Tattoos. I knew that certain tribes marked themselves in this way. This man was no Indian, though.

"He insulted my good name, Blue Sam," Ben grumbled.

"Save it for the French, shipmate."

"I will have no more fighting in my tavern, you, you . . . Yankees! And abusing our valuable ratter, our sweet little dog! Have you no heart, man?" yelled Mrs. Walker. She gave Ben a great whack with her broom. "This is a civilized place. Behave in a gentlemanly fashion or leave!"

"Come then, shipmate," Blue Sam laughed. "This place is too grand for the likes of us . . . Yankees."

"Cross the street when you see me coming, you piece of Halifax dung," Ben snarled at me. Then he snatched up his tricorne, clapped it on his head and followed Blue Sam out the door.

"Sweet little dog?" I mumbled.

"Yankee sailors!" groaned Baldish, ignoring me. "What have things come to? A Boston hothead and a blue giant. If there's any justice in this world, those boys are on *Squirrel* and not on *Pembroke*."

"You'll find out in the morning," I said.

"And I will be relieved to return to *Pembroke*, hotheads and blue men or not. Join me, William. You would make a good sailor. Consider it. Think of the jolly times we would have if you would only volunteer."

I had long ago given up any idea of being a sailor. My future was on dry, solid land. "War does not sound very appealing to me, Baldish."

"War is simple. Follow orders and kill the French. Take their strongholds, as we did at Louisbourg last year. And drive them out the way we did after Louisbourg was ours and we were raiding along the Gaspé. Simple, see? It is life ashore that is complicated. Besides, you have no love for the French, do you?"

I thought about that as I walked back to my small room at Mr. Bushell's printing office later that night. I had lived and worked there since my father's death from smallpox the year before. King Louis padded ahead of me as I considered the idea of becoming a sailor.

But what did I need with leaky boats? Here in Halifax I had work as an inker, food in my belly,

17

and a warm place to sleep. Here I would not be shot or scalped or drowned. I might be punched now and then, but that was to be expected in rough inns and taverns. No. Life was better in Halifax — quiet, uneventful and safe.

That is what I told myself just before I fell asleep, King Louis's harsh snoring rumbling in my ears. And I almost believed it.

* * *

Mr. Bushell wakened me near midnight, crying out that a building was burning. I threw on clothing and dashed to join our fellow members of the Hand in Hand firefighting club. We rushed out of the printing office into the cold night, buckets in our hands. To my horror, the fire was at the house where Baldish lived when not aboard ship. We scrambled to help the other firefighters already at work. The fire must be put out before it spread to other buildings.

Smoke poured from the open doorway and rolled against the windows' glass. I worked mindlessly, willing the fire to die. Bucket after bucket passed to me. I swung each one on, sweat pouring down my face. Then I saw it. A palm against one of the panes. I will never be able to explain this, but I knew it was Baldish.

Someone tried to hold me back. The words *Fool!*

Stop! They are all out! held no meaning at all. I broke free, ignoring the shouts and warnings and the heat of the fire as I ran in. All I could think of was finding Baldish and dragging him out before the roof collapsed. I recall reaching him and starting to tug at his hands . . . and then nothing more.

I did get him out, though. I learned that, before I came to again, others took Baldish away to the Hospital for Hurt and Sick Seamen, since his hands and face were burned. In a few more hours the house was no more than smouldering rubble. When they pulled the blackened body of a dead man from the ashes, the sight and smell of it made my stomach roil. But I swallowed hard and struggled to act bravely. Mr. Bushell and I returned to the office. We were greeted by his anxious daughter, but Miss Elizabeth knew better than to ask us for details. Our workday would begin soon enough.

I fell back onto my bed, not bothering to undress. I have never been much for praying, but I said a prayer of thanks for Miss Elizabeth. Given her father's fondness for drink, the press might not have run without her. I said a second prayer for the dead man. Then I prayed that I would never again see such a terrible sight as that burned, twisted corpse.

The next evening, I visited Baldish at the hospital. Although a young man of perhaps twenty, he had surprisingly little hair. What remained after last night's near escape was quite singed. Still, he was in good spirits, although sorry that his return to *Pembroke* would be delayed.

"Who will bring the newspaper out to Mr. Cook next Monday?" he asked. "The ship's master cannot live without his *Halifax Gazette* every week."

"I can do that," I assured him. "It will give me a chance to see *Pembroke*."

Next Monday afternoon I walked down to the ferry wharf. A man was blowing on the conch shell he used to summon passengers for the trip over to Dartmouth. I told his crew that my destination was *HMS Pembroke*, and paid the fare. In I leapt, joining a group of shivering people and a hen that had puffed itself up against the cold until it filled its cage like a burst pillow. Someone in the ferry broke wind thunderously. That caused everyone except the chicken and its mistress to laugh as though this were the funniest thing they had heard all day. Perhaps it was.

Sailors cast off the lines. They raised the sail and the ferry surged across the harbour. Icy spray splashed over the bow and us. Finally the crew eased the ferry up to the ship's side.

I shouted up to anyone who might care to listen. It appeared that someone did, for a wool-capped head fringed with frizzy, grey hair popped into sight. A rope ladder dropped down the ship's side. I caught hold of it and carefully mounted its wooden steps.

The wool-capped head belonged to an old sailor who introduced himself as Tom Pike.

"Poor Baldish," he said. "Lucky for him you came along though, eh? Otherwise he would've been cooked like a suckling pig."

Mr. Pike offered to show me the way to Mr. Cook, and led me across the deck and opened a door. "We must pass through the bowels of the ship to get to the captain's cabin. Mr. Cook is working there. Mind the rats. After this hard winter we do have our share of the beasties."

It seemed as though he truly meant bowels. As we made our way down the stairs, the smell began to take on a life of its own. There was a mixture of unwashed sailors and dirty bilge water. The ghosts of a hundred meals of boiled salt beef haunted the shadows. I did not know whether to breathe through my mouth or through my nose. I was considering not breathing at all, when we finally left the smell behind. Tom Pike rapped at a closed door. We were told to enter.

The cabin was a spacious and comfortable place. Mr. Cook leaned over a chart, his palms flat on the table, studying what was drawn there. He raised his eyes. I fear I babbled then. I went on about Baldish, the fire and my work at the printing house.

Mr. Cook accepted the newspaper. "Pity about Sykes. He's a good man, a good sailor. With luck he will heal quickly. And you are?"

"Jenkins, sir. William Jenkins. Baldish is very fond of *Pembroke*, sir. I know he longs to be back on her. He often says I should volunteer."

"So you should, a healthy young man such as you. Make your family proud."

"I have no family, sir."

"Think of your king and country, then. If you wish to serve good King George, join us. We are short-handed in this war with the French, and things will heat up in a few weeks. Have you sailed before?"

"A little, sir, as a passenger on *Alderney* when we came over from Plymouth. And a number of times with my father when he was a merchant seaman." I hesitated, and then added, "We used to go up to Louisbourg to make deliveries of rum for Mr. Mauger."

"Ah, yes. Louisbourg is a magnificent town.

Ours now, of course. If your father was a sailor, it's in your blood, then. Do you read and write?"

"Yes, sir. I also do sums. And I speak some French."

"There you are. French will be a most useful thing, I believe, once we have won this war. We want good men, loyal fighting men. But a man with a bit of education and a touch of ambition may go places in the navy."

"I have never thought of it that way, sir."

He looked up and smiled a bit. "This opportunity to serve is as clear as . . . well, the ink on your fingers."

Baldish had been nagging at me since *Pembroke* had arrived last fall. Soldiers in taverns had coaxed me to enlist. But I believe it was Mr. Cook's words that finally moved me.

Chapter 4
April 27, 1759

And so it was that I found myself again standing on the ferry wharf, a canvas seabag over my shoulder. In it were the few pieces of clothing that I owned, and Father's spyglass. A scabby but cheerful Baldish Sykes was there. So were two of his shipmates who had also been taken to hospital.

"You are certain, William?" asked Mrs. Walker cautiously. She, Miss Elizabeth and Mr. Bushell had accompanied me to say farewell. King Louis, though, was locked in the printing office so that he would not try to leap into the ferry. "I promised your father that I would be responsible for you," Mrs. Walker went on. "I am not certain that giving my blessing on this matter is a wise thing."

"Nonsense, Mrs. Walker," said Mr. Bushell. "It is the nature of a young man to seek adventure."

"He'll get plenty of that on *Pembroke*," whispered Baldish to his shipmates. "Scrubbing decks and hauling lines are the very soul of adventure." They all snorted. At least until Mrs. Walker gave them a dark look.

"This is for you, William," Mr. Bushell continued, handing me a small, cloth-covered book. "It is a journal. See that you write in it daily, if possible. When you return I may publish some of your adventures in the *Gazette*. My readers will be hungry for an honest account of the war."

"Thank you, sir."

I shook his hand and shouted, "Farewell, my friends!" Then I added, "Give my best to King Louis!"

"William, only you would pass on good wishes to a dog," laughed Miss Elizabeth.

I watched them grow smaller and smaller as the ferry took us out. Act like a sailor, I told myself firmly, giving them one last hearty wave. Then I turned my back on Halifax and my face towards *Pembroke*. There was my future.

Once aboard the ship, Baldish took me to the purser, Mr. Wise. One of his jobs was to enter me into the muster book that contained all the names of the ship's company. I scanned the well-worn ledger as he wrote. The pages told where and when each man had joined, what he was to be paid, and, if it happened, the date of his death. *Landsman*, he wrote beside my name, since I had little actual naval experience, despite my dozen trips on the *Merry Lot*. Eighteen shillings a month and food would be my pay. I was assigned to the same mess and watch as Baldish, which meant we would share meals and work together.

"You will serve on this ship until the end of the campaign this fall, God willing. Then you will be free to return here to Halifax or go to the colonies with the other volunteers from down there," said Mr. Wise. "And a promise of no impressment."

That was something. Often enough men were forced into service when a press gang would ask a poor fellow if he would like to volunteer and, when he said no, drag him onto their ship anyway.

Baldish took me below to the gun deck where we would sleep and eat. There he showed me where to put my seabag and my shoes, since I would not be needing shoes on board. Then we hurried back up. If I worked hard and learned what needed to be learned, Baldish explained, there was the possibility of advancement to the next position on the ship, which was ordinary seaman. That would mean one shilling more a month. If I persevered and survived, I might even reach the rank of able seaman. But that would take years of training, Baldish admitted.

"Welcome to *Pembroke*, William Jenkins," said Tom. "And welcome home to you, Baldish. I see you still have a few bits of hair left on that shiny head of yours."

"Help Tom Pike and those others," a passing officer snapped. "Step quickly. There are barrels to be brought aboard."

For the rest of that day, I could have been in another country where people spoke a language I had never before heard! It did begin to come back to me, though. Fore and aft, larboard, starboard. Cutter instead of boat, and belay instead of stop. You did not tie something down with a line. You made it fast. A sailor was a tar. It made my head spin fast enough, I have to admit. The navy had a language all its own, and if it had not been for Baldish and Tom, I would have drowned in it. Tom had appointed himself my sea daddy. He would show me the ropes, he explained, which was very important.

I am not certain how many of the ropes I learned that day. There were miles and miles of line on *Pembroke*, and every inch of it had a purpose. Naturally, each rope had an odd name — hawser, brail, sheet and halyard. Some were thick and others thin, but all were made from the same coarse hemp. I pulled until my hands blistered, and then I pulled more. There was nothing to do but pull away until all the barrels brought out to us had been hauled onto the ship. Then they must be taken down below and stored somewhere out of the way.

All of us were at work at the same time, which meant there were hundreds of men and boys doing one thing or another. To the gulls overhead we must have looked like a warren of frantic rabbits. Now and again I would bump into another sailor. Most of them laughed in understanding, but a few grumbled, calling me a landlubber.

"It won't be so bad when we're at sea," said Baldish.

"I won't be a landlubber then?" I asked.

"You'll still be a landsman," he answered. "But unless all hands are called on deck, it will be less crowded. We'll be part of the larboard watch, you see."

I began to ask him just what *was* a larboard watch, but then one of the officers ordered us to help take bread below. Two hundred loaves had been brought aboard.

"Aye, sir!" shouted Baldish.

A heavy bag of loaves in each of my hands, I followed Baldish as he wove a path amongst the men. At least no line pulling was involved. *Pembroke* was far larger than *Merry Lot*, and so had more decks. There was the main deck, which served as an upper gun deck. Below that was the lower gun deck, then the orlop deck, and finally the hold. Down we went into the ship, down and towards the stern until we reached the bread room. It was lined with tin.

"Keeps out the rats — two-legged as well as four-legged," Baldish told me with a wink. "Sailors do love their bread, whether it is soft bread or ship's bread. All the rum is locked up as well, since we love it even more."

Trip after trip we made, until I almost wished I had a line to pull. It was not a wish I should have made, because before I could take a breath — all the bread was locked away now — I was pulling once more. There was water to bring aboard, after all, and no time to waste. Sweat ran into my eyes, but I could not let go of the line to wipe it away, so I shrugged my shoulder across my face. Finally the cask was on the deck and we had a moment's rest.

"Pick up my chest!" a young officer shouted at two sailors. "Pick it up and take it below, I say."

"We have carried your chest down and then up again," grumbled one of the sailors carrying it.

"Can't make up his bloody mind," muttered the other sailor, his look sullen.

I swear the entire deck fell silent. All I could hear was the creaking of the ship as it strained against its anchor.

"Marines!" shouted the officer. "Put these men in irons!"

"Yes, sir," a red-coated soldier answered.

The two sailors were driven away at musket point by a group of marines. I already knew that these soldiers were assigned to each of the king's ships to keep the peace and prevent mutinies. We watched the sailors stumble below, and then everyone seemed to give a sigh, and work began again. Finally someone blew a signal on a whistle.

"Supper!" cheered Baldish, rubbing his hands.

This time I would be eating the bread rather than carrying it. I thought I could hear hundreds of rumbling stomachs, but maybe it was just my own. It was making enough noise for ten.

"This is our table," Baldish told me once we were below. "It hangs right here between Savage Billy and Deadly Raker. Billy is our . . ."

I began to ask him why the cannons had been given names, but the words did not come out. All I could do was stare at the table, or rather who was seated there. It was Blue Sam and Boston Ben.

"Just my luck," said Ben. "I have you to thank for this, Blue Sam. I said we should join *Squirrel*, but no. It had to be *this* tub. And now here I am, stuck with this worthless piece — "

"Tub?" The speaker was a small old man carrying an enormous pot. He slammed it down upon the table and then sat down. "Did I hear him call

our dear *Pembroke* a tub, Mr. Pike?" It was some-
what hard to understand him, since he had no
teeth.

"You did, Gum Well," Tom replied. "Now, who
shall have this?" he said, beginning to dish out the
food.

I would learn in time that Tom Pike was a man
of great influence. He was Mr. Wise's favourite
cousin. As purser, Mr. Wise controlled the ship's
supplies. Displease the purser's cousin, and perhaps you would not get your proper rations. I
believe it was the only thing that saved me from
being beaten to mush by Boston Ben just then. He
must have loved his food even more than the idea
of punching me.

"I misspoke. I am filled with joy to be here,"
said Ben joylessly. But it satisfied Tom, and so he
began to serve out the food until all seven of us
had a bowl of salt fish soup, a chunk of cheese,
a large piece of bread and a tankard of beer. I sat
down on one of the benches at the table that hung
by lines from the ceiling. "Will Captain Simcoe
have us exercise the guns this evening, do you
think, Tom?" asked a little boy.

"I expect so, Davy," Tom answered. His food finished, he placed a pipe in his mouth, although he
did not light it. "No smoking below," he explained

to me. "No smoking and no open flame. Keep it in mind, William Jenkins."

"I will. I do not smoke, though."

"A sailor who does not smoke?" laughed Mr. Well, showing his pink gums. "We shall correct that in time, or my name is not Gum Well."

Gum Well, Blue Sam — I supposed they were no odder names than Capitaine Rosbif, Vairon's name for me.

"Which gun is ours?" asked Blue Sam.

"Savage Billy," said Davy with pride. "I am the powder-boy."

"And a good fast one he is," said Gum Well.

My stomach full, I was beginning to relax and look forward to my bed, wherever it might be. That was when someone began to beat a drum and an officer shouted, "Clear for action!"

Plates, spoons and bowls were gathered up. Tables and benches were stowed away.

"Get to it, William!" snapped Baldish. "Nothing can be in the way when the guns are fired."

An officer named Lieutenant Robson shouted out commands. Tom gave me the task of hauling on the tackle. In went a cartridge of gunpowder and a wad of old rope and canvas. No cannonballs were used, though, since we did not want to blow everything around us to bits. The cartridge was rammed in, the cannon was run out — no small job as it was exceedingly heavy — and the cannon was fired. And I was to mind my toes if I wanted to keep all ten of them. When a fully loaded cannon was fired during actual battle, the force of the blast would cause it to roll back violently. It was one of the reasons we had to clear for action.

Twice more we loaded and fired. Again and again the cannon roared as the gunpowder burned. Flames and foul-smelling white smoke shot out. Each blast shook the deck and shook me to my core. My eyes stung and my ears rang, but it didn't matter. I could imagine what battle would be like as each great gun boomed out, sending a shock through me. The officers shouted orders, the men swabbed out the guns to take care of stray sparks, loaded powder, put smouldering slow match to the touch hole. There was a flash, a tremendous boom, and the cannon leapt back. It all made my blood thrill and my hearing grow faint.

"Not bad," said Lieutenant Robson, "but not good enough. Not quick enough. We will want to speed things up, men, if we are going to bring Québec to her knees."

There was an hour or so of leisure afterwards, and I used the time to write in the journal Mr. Bushell had given me. I had no pen or ink, but I did have an old brass leadholder, which I suppose made more sense. Ink could spill. I opened the journal and wrote the date at the top of the first page. *April 27, 1759.* What to write, though?

"Beginning a great book?" teased Baldish.

"It will be a rousing tale of all my adventures," I said. "Not sure where to start, though."

"Begin with *Pembroke*," said Baldish with a jaw-creaking yawn. "I shall even help you with it, since I know her inside and out."

I wrote what he told me, or as much as I could get down:

HMS Pembroke *is a new ship that was launched at Plymouth in 1757. She weighs 1222 tons, is 156 feet in length, and 42 feet at the beam width. She carries an assortment of guns. The marines have their small arms, muskets and such. We have our cannons and, when necessary, pikes and axes. There are 26 of the twenty-four-pound great gun variety, so named because they shoot twenty-four-pound balls. Savage Billy is the best of those. There are 26 twelve-pounders, and 10 six-pounders.* Pembroke *may carry 420 sailors and officers, as well as 67 marines.*

I asked Baldish if we had our full complement of sailors. He said we have fewer than those numbers right now, but that we still have the French shaking in their pretty little shoes.

At that I started laughing too hard to write, and so I left it for another time. Still, it seemed to me like a good start. We prepared to retire, which meant we hung our hammocks — slinging is how the sailors put it — so that each of us had 14 inches of sleeping space. It took several tries and several falls before I was able to get into my hammock. My messmates were greatly amused, naturally. Once in, I lay there as though I had been turned to stone, afraid that I would roll out. I stared at the deck above me and listened to the snores. Sailors fell asleep instantly, I saw, in spite of the belches, wind breaking and snorts. There was no end to it! Wondering how I would ever be able to sleep with all the noise and the stink, I closed my eyes. I slept.

Chapter 5
End of April, 1759

The next day was mild and clear, and as work-filled as the one before it. There were decks to wash, breakfast to be eaten, and more supplies to be brought on board. And since the weather was fair, the order was given to loosen the sails so that they would dry. We could not have the canvas rotting.

"This is as good a time as any, Jenkins," said Tom. "Up you go. Show him how, Baldish."

We did as we were told. Up into *Pembroke's* rigging I climbed, clinging to the rope ladder. I must put my feet here, Baldish said, and hold on to this part only. I must not look down. I must not fall, lest I shame us both. I could not imagine how much shame I would feel if I were lying on the deck like a squashed toad, but I obeyed Baldish. And I tried very hard not to show how frightened I felt. Up we clambered, leaving the deck far below. Though Baldish had told me not to look down, only straight ahead, I did peek down once, and it was a mistake. The sight of men below, the size of mice, made my stomach clench and my hands sweat so much I nearly lost my grip. My foot slipped and I swung about wildly. I knew I was going to fall.

"Hold tight, William," urged Baldish. "Both feet on the ratlines. There you are, as good as can be."

His voice steadied me enough for me to catch my balance again. There I stood, so high up, feeling the breeze in my hair. A gull swooped past. I was in its world now.

When we reached the yard, a long, heavy stretch of wood where the mainsail was bundled, I was told to stop and watch. This I did willingly. Baldish and the others climbed out as nimbly as monkeys. They untied the sail and down it went, yards and yards of canvas. This is simple, I thought — nothing to it at all. I watched the sailors go from sail to sail, their feet certain on the lines, their movements confident. Below and beyond was Halifax. I could see tiny people moving along the streets, and I wondered if anyone could see me.

"Climb up whenever you get the chance," Baldish advised me when we were safely back on the deck. "The ship is quiet and steady here at anchor. It will be very different when we're at sea."

When we were all called to assemble on deck

the next morning, anyone wearing a hat or cap removed it. Then I caught sight of the two men who had been put in irons yesterday. Captain Simcoe read the charge of disobedience. Then he read the law the men had broken. Since they had disobeyed an officer, there was the possibility that they could be put to death, which seemed unbelievable to me. They had only refused to carry a sea-chest, after all!

Without moving his lips, Baldish whispered, "I can tell what you are thinking. Orders are orders, and punishment happens when they are not obeyed. But neither lad will swing today."

The two men were asked if they had anything to say. They did not. The captain ordered twelve lashes for each of them. The men's shirts were removed and the two sailors were tied over gun barrels. When Captain Simcoe said, "Bosun, do your duty," the bosun took the cat-o'-nine-tails out of its red cloth bag and shook loose its nine metal-tipped cords. It was, I knew, why sailors talked about letting the cat out of the bag. Mr. Thompson drew his fingers through the cords to lay them out and then began whipping the first man.

Twelve lashes do not sound like so very much, until you see what each lash can do. The first sailor somehow bore the flogging in silence. The second man screamed all through it — a terrible sound. When it was over, the men's backs were covered in sickening bloody stripes. My face must have shown what my stomach was feeling.

"The surgeon will see to them," Baldish assured me as they were taken below by their messmates.

After the flogging Tom went to see a friend of his who had been ill for a while, and I walked with him. We went down to the orlop deck and then worked our way through the ship. It was quite dark, since below the ship's waterline are no gun ports to let in light. Tom carried a lantern to light our way.

I did not envy the purser and Dr. Jackson working down there in the orlop; it smells of the huge piles of damp anchor line stored there. It is also where the doctor cares for sick and injured men. He was doing just that when we arrived, applying some sort of ointment to the back of one of the men who had been flogged. These two men were the liveliest of the patients. The other six simply lay there in their hammocks with their eyes closed. Whether they were asleep or awake, I could not tell. Tom leaned over his friend and spoke quietly to him. The fellow did not open his eyes, but he did manage to give a weak smile.

If I were flogged — and I vow I never will be — I would not be in such a happy mood. But the men who had been whipped laughed and joked as though they were at a picnic. Later Tom said that there is no point in holding grudges. Do your duty. Take the good with the bad, and face the day with a clear conscience.

Someone should mention this to Boston Ben. It will not be me, though.

The next morning, Sunday, we all changed into clean clothing. Those men with long pigtails braided one another's hair. Then we gathered on deck once more. Since *Pembroke* did not have a minister, Captain Simcoe spoke. Rather, he again read the rules, what I was told were the Articles of War. I realized that it would only be a matter of time before I made a mistake and broke one of those rules. The thought of that was not pleasant.

Neither was the fact that Tom's friend, the man we had visited yesterday, was dead. He had passed away in the night.

"Joseph Jones had been poorly for a while," said Gum Well. We were watching one of our boats take the dead man's body ashore for burial. "He will sleep in a snug grave in Halifax. Pity he did not get a chance to take a few Frenchmen with him, though."

"Not right," said Tom. "A sailor should be buried at sea. Wrap me up in my hammock, put a stitch through my nose, and a cannonball at my feet. That is all the burying I ever want."

"And the stitch through the nose would be for . . . " I ventured.

"Just to make good and certain you are truly dead," said Davy cheerfully. "Are you coming to watch the auction, William?"

"What auction?" I asked.

"Joseph's belongings, of course," said Davy, as though I should have known such a thing.

It seemed unfeeling to me at first that a dead man's possessions should be sold and he not even in his grave yet. But I supposed it was practical. When *Pembroke* returned to England in time, his family would get what money was raised.

I had little time to dwell on stitches, noses or auctions, though. Each morning the sun rose, bringing with it all the work involved in readying the ship to sail. Some of it was already completed. *Pembroke*'s upper masts and the crosspieces they called yards had spent the long winter lying on the deck covered in grease. All of those yards and masts had been cleaned and set back in their proper positions.

We were like bees in a hive, all buzzing away at

our toil. The carpenter and his helpers made small repairs to the ship's boats. The sailmaker and his fellows spent endless hours making certain that every sail was in good repair, while the armourer and his assistants hammered away at anything metal that needed seeing to. Boats filled with supplies came and went all day long. I helped bring on more water, carried wood below, and stowed food in the hold. Because I was only a landsman they were common enough tasks, things I had done ashore, but here it seemed different. Here I was part of a ship, a member of the crew. Here I was a Pembroke. As for the captain, he had other duties, and one of them was entertaining the general who commanded the soldiers here at Halifax.

The routine of fixing and mending was broken one day, though, when General James Wolfe came on board *Pembroke*. It caused a great deal of commotion, enough that I wrote about it in my journal that night. You would have thought the king himself was coming to call. When the general's barge neared our ship, Mr. Thompson took a deep breath. "Man the side!" he shrieked.

I had no idea what he meant, but others did, and so we sailors lined up to receive the general as he came aboard. Mr. Thompson blew a series of notes on a silver whistle he wears around his neck, and General Wolfe was piped aboard.

"Grand, ain't it?" whispered Baldish without moving his lips. He had quite a talent for it.

I only caught a glimpse of General Wolfe, and noticed nothing special. My father used to say that greatness is not something that can always be seen. It is true enough regarding General Wolfe, who is small and delicate looking with bright red hair and a pointed nose. He coughed a fair deal and kept a handkerchief over his mouth. And he walked as though his bones hurt, like an old man would, although he seemed not much more than thirty years of age.

Later Baldish said he had heard that it was a good thing James Wolfe had chosen the army rather than the navy — it seems he nearly vomited himself to pieces when sailing from England.

At least I am not cursed with that problem.

* * *

The first day of May dawned fine and clear. It was celebrated with a good deal of enthusiasm. Vice Admiral Saunders — he commands the entire navy — saluted Rear Admiral Durell with fifteen guns. Admiral Durell then saluted Admiral Saunders with fifteen guns. The garrison made their noisy salute, and then we fell to our work.

Later that day it occurred to me that I was being

given any truly unpleasant bit of work that could be found. I was certain when I was sent to clean the heads. I had once been an emptier of chamber pots when I lived at Mrs. Walker's inn, and that had been unpleasant enough. But there were no chamber pots on *Pembroke*, only two boards with holes cut into them, near the bow of the ship. At any time of day or night, sailors went up to the bow and used the heads when nature called, and they weren't always so careful with their aim. Smeared with filth, the heads smelled worse than any chamber pot. With more than three hundred of us using them . . .

I do not envy Captain Simcoe's responsibility regarding this ship. I do, however, envy the fact that he has his own private head just off his cabin.

I began to feel a restlessness filling *Pembroke*. The sailors were eager to go to sea and leave Halifax in their wake. They were keen to blaze a trail for the rest of the navy and army.

"I was aboard *Lenox* when we captured the Spanish ship *Princesa* back in forty," said Gum, his voice filled with pride.

"Sixteen forty?" asked Davy, smirking.

Gum gave him a small whack. "Seventeen forty, my lad. Now *that* was as fine an adventure as you could want, with three fine British ships — *Orford*,

Lenox and *Kent* — chasing down the prize. Our poor captain had his hand shot off, but did that stop him from leading us? It did not!"

"It is our squadron that will lead the way this time," Tom explained. "Mr. Cook draws an excellent chart, and it is an excellent chart of the St. Lawrence we must have if this navy is to get up to Québec. There will be buoys to set out for the other ships to mark a safe way, and no end of important tasks, lads! We cannot have our ships running aground."

"What about General Wolfe and his army?" I asked. "What about Admiral Saunders and the rest of the ships?"

"They will follow in time," Tom told me.

Any day now, the men said, and it seemed they were correct. On the 4th of May there was an attempt to leave the harbour, but there was so much loose ice floating around, the idea was abandoned. By the next morning, though, the wind had shifted. *Pembroke* seemed to shiver with excitement. I could almost feel it when I put my hand on one of her stays.

It took almost the entire crew to ready *Pembroke*. Some sailors scrambled up and into the rigging. They would handle the sails. I was ordered to help pull up the anchor. It was a job for those who had no real sailing skills, and so for the moment it suited me perfectly. Round and round dozens of us walked while pushing against the bars of the capstan. Up came the anchor as the line very slowly wound up. If this had been *Merry Lot*, every man would have been singing a sea shanty to help the work along. Not on this vessel. Grunts and groans were the only sounds we made, since the navy believed that singing during work was bad for morale. Whether that was right or wrong, it did not matter. An hour later, the anchor was secured in place.

A command was given to make sail. Down came the yards and yards of canvas and as the wind filled them, *Pembroke* began to move. It must have been a wonderful sight for anyone on shore who happened to be watching our thirteen vessels set sail at the same time. *Pembroke* was grand, but of course Rear Admiral Durell's flagship *Princess Amelia* was even grander and larger. The ensign snapped smartly on every ship. On the admiral's, though, a long pennant also flew high above its deck. We left the harbour behind, passing by Cornwallis Island and Cape Sambro.

Farewell, Halifax, I thought. Farewell!

From that morning everything changed. The crew was divided into two watches, and each was further divided into sections according to where they would work on the ship. *Pembroke* became a fighting machine and every one of us was a moving part in that machine.

Davy and the other boys ran errands, cleaned, carried powder in battle and helped to look after the livestock. I was amazed to see just how many animals were on *Pembroke*. Most, like the calves, sheep and ducks, would end up on the captain's table. The goat and chickens provided him with milk and eggs.

"Always test the wind," Davy advised me as he tossed the animals' manure over the side. "Calf flops are all well and good, but you don't want them sailing back at you!"

Boston Ben, Baldish, Bob Carty and Blue Sam were experienced topmen, the pride of *Pembroke*. They spent most of their watch far up above the ship's deck, where they handled the sails. Tom and Gum had once been topmen, but now they were too old and stiff for the dangerous tasks. Instead they worked on the forecastle deck. So did I, in spite of the fact that I had so little real experience. The bosun would scream an order — Mr. Thompson had a very loud voice — and we would all jump to action. If Tom and Gum had not been there to explain what the order meant, I might have been flogged for disobedience.

"We shall make a fine forecastleman of you in good time," vowed Tom.

I admit I wondered about that. There was little time for wondering, though. The bosun and the other officers had no end of tasks for us to do, and Tom usually found other chores for me that he thought would help my training.

We rose early to clean the ship. I coiled lines, touched up paint and swabbed decks. All this we did to the sound of the ship's bell being rung every half hour. There had been none of this going on when I sailed with my father years ago. "One bell means the first half hour of the watch is done," Tom explained. "Two bells are for the next half hour. When you hear eight bells, your watch is over, and you have four hours to yourself. Four hours on and four off. The same with the dog watches, which are two hours long."

"Only four hours for sleep?" I asked.

"Only four when we are at sea," laughed Gum. "Unless the call for all men on deck is given. You will learn to sleep where and when you can."

We were again surrounded by chunks of ice. Even the lookouts high up in the rigging could not see empty water. I had not needed to be told how dangerous our situation was, since I could see it on the faces of the officers. Ice had sunk many a ship out here. Mr. Cook was often on the deck, speaking with the captain or studying the ice. I wondered if he noticed that I was here on the ship. But I did not ask him. A common sailor never spoke to the officers unless spoken to, since they were gentlemen and we were not. That afternoon, though, Mr. Cook sent for me. Back I went down the length of the ship, and up the flight of stairs that led to the quarterdeck. I had not yet set foot there, since it was for officers and officers in training only — almost as sacred as the captain's cabin!

"There you are, Jenkins," said Mr. Cook. "I was pleased to learn that you decided to serve your king after all." Then he turned to Captain Simcoe. "Sir, this is the young fellow I mentioned last night at supper."

The captain wiped his forehead with the back of his hand. To me, he did not look well. "Mr. Cook says you read and do sums very handily. And you speak some French. He thinks you should have signed on as a midshipman."

How Ben laughed when I repeated the captain's words that night. He nearly choked on his bread. "*You* a midshipman? Takes a gentleman to be a midshipman, and you are as much a gentleman as I am married to a mermaid."

49

"Now, now," said Bob. "That would not be entirely true. Did Mr. Cook himself not come from humble beginnings? Yes, he did. His father was a simple farm labourer, but Mr. Cook worked hard and now he's a ship's master."

"He is indeed," agreed Gum. "Some day he will be a captain. Mark my words." He smiled and showed me his pink gums. "Who can say what is in store for you, young Jenkins."

What was in store for all of us was weather as mixed as weather could be. We had fog, then gales of winds. And always there was ice. It rained so hard that I could scarcely see the other ships, and so to make certain of their locations, we stayed in contact. Admiral Durell had a cannon fired every two hours. Some of our sailors answered back by firing muskets. A few times the lookout called that a ship had been sighted. We would all stare into the distance, trying to make out whether or not it was the enemy. If so, there could be fighting. I had never seen a battle at sea, much less been in one. The practice with our great gun Savage Billy had given me some idea of what it would be like, though. I only hoped I would be as brave as I thought I was.

The foul weather made working on deck a misery. It also made it far more dangerous. With the ship leaning far over, and sea water running down the deck, we had to take great care not to be swept away. There were more injuries than usual — a twisted ankle here and a wrenched shoulder there. The doctor was kept busy seeing to the injured.

I suffered a knock on the head one day when *Pembroke* slid down a wave and I tumbled down the companionway steps. It was only a lump, though, nothing to keep me from my duties.

When our watch was over, I began to ask Tom about what being in battle was like, when Ben gave a terrifying shriek. "Rats!" he cried in horror. "Right here under our table! How can a man eat his dinner with that going on?"

Baldish looked down. "There is no rat," he said to Ben. "Not unless there is one in its belly."

I laughed aloud. "Why, it's King Louis!"

He whined and licked my leg while I scratched behind his ears.

"A stowaway," laughed Baldish. "And I thought you were a clever dog, King Louis. Only a fool would stow away on a ship of war."

"Your dog, is he?" Gum asked me.

"I suppose he is, if he is anyone's at all," I said. "How did you get here, old friend?" I murmured as I petted him.

"Perhaps he came out on one of the supply

boats," Davy suggested, and that was when King Louis jumped up on the table.

"Get that filthy tavern dog away from my food or I will heave the creature overboard!" shouted Ben.

King Louis's ears flattened against his head. He growled like a small lion and leaped over Ben's plate. Off he dashed, the last of Ben's salt pork in his mouth. Ben cursed and raged, but his anger was drowned out by the howls of laughter coming from his shipmates.

"Bested by a little beast," teased Tom.

"Keep it away from me, Jenkins," Ben warned me. "I will drown it as soon as look at it."

But Ben did not have to look at King Louis at all. Louis stayed in the hold battling the rats. There were a thousand places that he could hide, which was why he had been able to conceal himself for so long. Sometimes he came out on deck to bask in the sun, but he always stayed well out of anyone's way. At night he stole in and I would pick him up and place him in my hammock. I often fell asleep to the sound of his snoring.

"Good old King Louis," I would whisper. "You needed an adventure too."

On and on we went, in good weather and bad, tacking back and forth, back and forth, until I was almost dizzy from it.

One morning someone said that he could see an island in the distance. I squinted out at the small, low bit of land, but it meant nothing to me. In fact, I had no idea at all where we were.

"Well, that is Bird Island," said Tom, "so Cape Breton Island is over there behind it. And Newfoundland is northeast of us. All the icebergs you would ever want pass by Newfoundland. Not this small stuff, but mountains of ice."

I tried to imagine it while I worked beside him and the others hauling on a line to pull up yet another sail. I had seen small ice islands back at Halifax, but nothing that looked like a mountain.

"That would be something," I said. "We could sail right up to it and take chunks to keep us cool on hot days." A fleeting memory of the ice house and Louisbourg slipped into my head. And with that of course came the image of Vairon.

"You'd never want to sail up to an ice mountain," grunted Tom. "One of those will tear the guts out of a ship."

"Then down you go to meet Davy Jones?" I asked.

"Do not think that, much less say it," whispered Gum with a shiver. "You might bring bad luck to this ship. Then *you* would be a Jonah and treated by the others as though you were not even here."

The next day our sailors dropped a signal flag to half-mast. I was told that it meant we needed a surgeon. *Pembroke*'s cutter was launched, and Mr. Cook was rowed over to Admiral Durell's ship *Princess Amelia*. When he returned, it was with the admiral's captain of marines and another man. They were met by our Dr. Jackson.

"It is Dr. John, the surgeon from *Prince of Orange*," whispered Tom. "They say Captain Simcoe is very ill. Must be if he needs two doctors."

The ship settled into nervous and respectful silence for the sake of our sick captain. Rumours flew around *Pembroke* like the gulls that often circled the ship. No one knew just how he fared, though, until the next day when all hands were called on deck.

"Pneumonia has taken Captain Simcoe," Mr. Cook told the crew solemnly. "He has departed this life."

Our vessels anchored near an island called Anticosti on the 17th of May, with every ensign and pennant flying at half-mast. All hands were once again called to the deck for the funeral. I could see Cape Gaspé in the distance, and I knew that somewhere beyond it flowed the St. Lawrence. Mr. Cook's voice droned on as he read the service. I should have listened closely out of respect, but all I could think of was that river. It would be our road to Québec and war.

There was a splash. I cringed a little at the sound of Captain Simcoe's corpse hitting the water. They had dropped his remains out of one of the gunroom ports. Weighed down with lead balls, the captain's body sank immediately. A cannon fired just then. There was a half minute or so of silence, and another boomed out. Twenty in all, a fitting farewell for an officer. That done, we all set sail once again, leaving the captain's remains behind in the gulf's cold water.

The event stayed with me, though, as I worked on deck. It was there when I ate my dinner and later took to my hammock to get what sleep I could. Two men dead and we have not even seen battle yet, I thought. Surely that will be the end of such bad business. It moved me enough that I recorded it all in my journal the next day.

I was wrong. No one could explain how it happened. For days there was little wind, and *Pembroke* was sliding over the water, her sails barely filled. There we stood among the chicken coops, which had been brought up so that the hens might get fresh air. The sun shone brightly, and all of us were sweating. It would be grand for the topmen up in the rigging, though.

Tom was showing me how to tie a bowline, saying that it was the perfect knot. "It never tightens too much, and it will never come loose by itself," he said. "Now you try it."

I took the line and began, repeating the words he had used to help me recall just how to tie the knot. "The rabbit runs out of the hole," I whispered to myself. "It goes around the tree, and back down the hole." I held out my effort. It did not look much like a bowline.

"Your rabbit has tangled himself up something awful," said Tom with a laugh.

At that moment, someone screamed and there was a tremendous splash.

"Man overboard!" shouted Baldish from above us. "Bob Carty's in the water! Throw something to him!"

At Mr. Cook's order the sails were dropped. I flung down the line, grabbed a hen coop and tossed it over the side. Many of us crowded the rail. There was nothing to see except the hen in her coop floating on the water. *Pembroke*'s cutter was launched and the men searched and searched, but nothing was found. They rescued the bedraggled hen and hoisted the cutter back onto the ship. The sea had swallowed up Bob Carty the same way it had swallowed Captain Simcoe.

"Fell like a rock," said Blue Sam that night.

"Sank like one, too," Boston Ben added. "Carty never stood a chance once the sea had him."

"Perhaps he lost consciousness when he hit the water," I suggested. I passed down a bit of salt beef to King Louis, who was crouched near my feet. "If that had not happened, he might have survived."

"Not likely," said Sam. "Carty could not swim. I can, but few among us are able to." He smiled. "You did a good deed in throwing out the hen coop, though, Jenkins. It was quick thinking — worthy of a sailor. Carty would have liked that."

"Bad things come in threes, and so that is the end of it," said Tom. "Three is enough for any butcher's bill."

"Let's have a song for Bob Carty!" shouted Gum. He dug an old fiddle from his battered sea-chest, and began to tune it. "'Spanish Ladies' was Bob's favourite. He did have an eye for the ladies."

We sang and my spirits lifted a little, especially after Sam's words. He thought of me as a fellow sailor, and that meant something. Bad things come in threes, I reminded myself. Perhaps we would have good things for a while.

And the music was good. I knew that sailors liked a good shanty. And they liked to dance. Gum played his fiddle and the men sang and clapped

to "Spanish Ladies," then to "Yankee Doodle" —
that at Ben's insistence — and then to "Over the
Hills and Far Away." I was filled with a sense of
good things coming.

It seemed to be so. The next day, the 19th of
May, the admiral's ship captured a French vessel
that was headed to Québec. Up the St. Lawrence
we went, struggling against the current. The wind
had to be just right, or else we would have been
swept back.

The St. Lawrence began to narrow a bit. Small
islands and the mouths of other rivers slid by, but
we explored none of them. It was slow going, not
just because of the current, but because the river
was unfamiliar. If there were sandbars, we could
run aground. If there were rocks, we might hit
one and sink. Each evening the ships anchored,
since it would have been impossible to continue
up the river in the dark. I felt myself slowly
becoming accustomed to *Pembroke*'s ways. Sleep
in the middle of the day came no easier. But the
navy's language and strange terms now made
more sense, and I thought that perhaps in time
I might become a proper tar. Still, I could not
keep myself from wondering about what we were
doing.

We passed by miles and miles of the Canadians'

countryside. Even without my spyglass I could see tidy villages along the shores. The spires of churches rose above them, putting me in mind of lighthouses. As for the farms, they were strangely arranged. Ribbon farms, they are called, because of the long, narrow bands of property that run to the river, which is like a highway to these people.

It was a highway to us as well, but one that was carrying us along our path to war.

I thought of that when I peered at one of the farms with my glass. I saw a boy standing on the shore, a bucket in his hand. I could see his face well enough to read the relief that was there. *Keep going, Englishmen,* his expression seemed to be saying. *Leave us in peace.* There will be no peace at Québec, though, not until this war is over and it is ours.

* * *

A ship must have a commander. On the 27th of May, the admiral sent Captain Wheelock over from *Squirrel* to take charge of *Pembroke.* The next morning while we were holystoning the decks, I was ordered to go to the quarterdeck. Mr. Cook wished to speak to me. I set down my sandstone, relieved to have a break from the scrubbing, and stood up. No one said a word, but all eyes followed me. I knew I had done nothing wrong, but I could feel every man thinking otherwise.

"Now Jenkins is in for it," hissed Ben as I passed by him. "Twenty lashes, I would guess."

"Sir," I said quietly when I reached Mr. Cook. "You wanted to see me?"

"I do," said Mr. Cook sternly. "What is this?" he asked, pointing to the deck.

I looked down. There lay a small body part.

"I believe it is a rat's tail, sir."

"And how did it get here?" asked Captain Wheelock.

"I have no idea, sir." But I did have an idea, for there behind the captain sat King Louis.

"I, however, do know," said Mr. Cook. "It was a dog that brought it and dropped it at the captain's feet. What do you say to that, Jenkins?"

"Sorry, sir," I said faintly.

"Sorry for what?" growled Mr. Cook.

"Sorry for letting the dog out of the bag?" I suggested hopefully. The words had popped out of my mouth before I could stop them, and I knew I was doomed. Not a sound came from the men, and even Ben kept his lips pressed shut. King Louis, however, yawned and gave a loud belch. I shut my eyes in despair, but then a low chuckle made me open them. It was Mr. Cook who was chuckling, and so was Captain Wheelock. One by one the other officers joined in.

"Your dog, Jenkins, is doing us a great service," said Captain Wheelock. "My cook says there is scarcely a rat to be seen in the galley."

"King Louis does love a plump rat," I said, and this caused the captain and Mr. Cook to laugh even harder.

"Dog out of the bag," said Mr. Cook, wiping his eyes. "King Louis. That is rich. Back to work, Jenkins. Your noble dog is welcome aboard this ship, and woe the man who annoys him." And that is the last time Ben threatened King Louis.

A few afternoons later, Tom guided me up into the rigging. It will be easier this time, I thought — I did it before back in Halifax, after all. This time was different, though. A crisp breeze was blowing. As we climbed, the stronger the wind became, and the more we swayed from side to side. I clutched the shrouds so hard my knuckles went white. I prayed my hands would not get sweaty again and make me lose my grip. If I fell, my head would crack open like a melon. I would be buried at sea and be food for the fish.

It was not a pleasant thought, and so I banished it from my mind and concentrated on climbing. I was a sailor, after all! The higher I climbed, the more my respect grew for the topmen who clambered up here even in the worst storms. Finally

Tom helped me onto the topcastle, where the lookouts and sharpshooters stood. Baldish was there, a spyglass in his hand.

"That there is Coudre Island, and those that know say we are some fifty miles or so from the city of Québec. Have a look," he said, handing me the glass. It was larger than mine, and more powerful.

I pressed the glass against my eye, and leaned on the rail of the crow's nest to steady myself. I could see our ships.

"Well?" asked Tom.

I cleared my throat. "I see a cow . . . no, two cows, and . . . three pigs. No Frenchmen."

I could not have been more correct. All of our ships set their anchors. Boats took a large party of soldiers ashore, but all they found were farm animals. Every man, woman and child had fled when they saw us coming.

"That's a good sign," I said after supper that evening. My head was spinning a little, since we had been given wine — our beer was gone. We stood at ease looking down at the river. "Since the French have run off, this war may be over quickly."

Boston Ben made a rude noise, and shook his head at my terrible ignorance. "They were just farmers."

Blue Sam, though, gave us both a cold look. "Farmers? The Canadians are more than farmers. Battling French soldiers is one thing, but you will see how the Canadian farmers fight." He spat into the water, and the spittle was swept away. "And remember their Abenaki allies. I would watch my scalp if I were you fools." Then he went below.

Scalping was an ugly business, and not something only the Indians did. The French, English and Americans were also guilty of the practice. The very thought of it made my own scalp crawl.

"Blue Sam should know," said Ben with an unpleasant smile. "I would wager he has taken his share of scalps."

"What do you mean?" I asked.

"He was a captive. Where do you think he got the tattoos? The Abenaki took him years ago when he was a boy. He left of his own accord in time, but by then it was too late. He was one of them, more Indian than white. Do not make an enemy of Blue Sam if you want to live long. And if you are ever taken by the French or by the savages — there is no difference — do anything you can to survive. Forget honour. Lie, cheat, steal, kill!"

I had never heard Ben make such a long, passionate speech. And with that he left us.

Chapter 6
June 8, 1759

Admiral Durell ordered *Pembroke*, *Devonshire*, *Centurion* and *Squirrel*, along with three of the transport ships loaded with soldiers, to set sail. Captain Gordon on *Devonshire* would be in command. We were to go as far up the St. Lawrence as we could and find the fire ships the French had constructed. Those ships were just as dangerous as they sounded. When lit by the French, they would float down among our ships, setting them ablaze as well.

Ben's words about the French stayed with me throughout the next days as we moved slowly up the river towards Québec. They were definitely in my mind when we received a signal that all our small boats were to be launched with armed men in them. No one was certain about how deep the water was, and so the sailing masters would take soundings in a treacherous section of the river they called the Traverse. The boats would leave in the dark so that the French would not see them. They knew we were here, of course. For days they had been lighting signal fires on the shore.

One evening later in June, I was silently wishing the expedition good luck. The silence was broken when Mr. Cook called out, "You and your mess will come as well, Jenkins. A bit of fun will do you good."

I could not see how it would do me any good at all, but an order was an order. Our *fun* lasted for two nights. I would drop a lead-weighted line down, and up I would pull it. Mr. Cook then made a note of the depth for a chart he planned to draw. It was a wet, chilly business, and all the while I never stopped thinking about what might be watching us from the darkness. At any moment I expected Indians or Canadians to come leaping out from the trees.

I was not disappointed. On the second night, Mr. Cook was finally satisfied that the Traverse could be safely crossed. Just as we were rowing back to *Pembroke*, unearthly screams came out of the forest. I swear my blood ran as cold as ice. We rowed for our lives, Mr. Cook shouting encouragement. Arrows shot by my head, and one struck the side of the boat. There was a shriek when another slammed into Ben's shoulder. Back he pitched into the water. When the marines on our ship realized what was happening, musket balls began to whiz through the darkness from *Pembroke*. The Canadians fell back. We called Ben's name again and again, but there was no sound from him. Only the terrible war cries of the Indians answered back as we pulled for the ship.

"Likely drowned," muttered Baldish when we were back on *Pembroke*. "And that is a mercy. If he had been captured . . . "

"What would they do to him?"

"Use your imagination, William," said Gum. "The savages surely will."

That night I could not rid myself of the image of Ben falling into the water. I could not rid myself of the idea that we had acted in a cowardly manner to just row away from him. Unable to sleep, I left my hammock near dawn and went up on deck. Mist was rising off the water — the day was going to be very hot. Already men were in the rigging, loosening the sails so that they would dry. Boston Ben will never do that again, I told myself.

"Thinking about Ben?" asked Mr. Cook. He had come up alongside me. "What we did was necessary. A boat filled with men cannot be sacrificed to save just one. Ben would have known that."

"I understand that, sir. Maybe Baldish was right. Maybe drowning was a mercy compared to being captured. Think of the things he would have had to do to survive."

"Life is a precious thing," said Mr. Cook thoughtfully. "But there is also honour. Without honour, life is meaningless, Jenkins. Remember that."

"I will, sir." But I was not so certain Mr. Cook was correct.

"We must be of good cheer," he said almost to himself. "The Traverse has been sounded and the buoys set. We may now sail through safely, and the rest of the fleet and the transports will follow. Then General Wolfe's men may do their duty."

Over the next days, up until the end of June, that is what happened. Anyone watching from Québec or from the shore would have seen an almost endless parade of British ships of war. One by one we went through the Traverse as easily as could be. Some of the ships had captured French pilots. These men were forced to help navigate through the dangerous waters. Most of us did perfectly well on our own, and I could not help but feel a bit of pride. After all, I had helped with the sounding.

The French now had two large floating batteries, sailing barges on which they had placed cannons. One came very close to *Pembroke*. We could actually hear the men on it talking.

"What are they saying, William?" asked Tom.

"Are they praying to heaven that something may save them from us?" laughed Davy.

"No," I answered. "They're not praying at all. I am no gentleman, but I am gentleman enough not to repeat what they're saying." For the French were swearing at us most inventively.

This made everyone laugh. They were laughing still when Captain Wheelock ordered us to run out the great guns. Down we went as fast as we could, our feet pounding on the steps. Each crew heaved on their gun's tackle to run the cannon out of its port.

It was not even necessary to load the guns, as it turned out.

"They're setting sail!" Davy shouted. "Fare thee well and good riddance, you cowards!"

Our navy gave me comfort. What had begun as a mere thirteen vessels was now a fearful fleet of almost one hundred and fifty. There were the warships, some carrying as many as ninety cannons. There were smaller fighting vessels of all sizes armed with cannons, as well as short, powerful sea mortars used to attack targets on shore. We had our own fire ships too. I tried to imagine what the French and Canadians were thinking as this floating death came closer and closer to a large island called Île d'Orléans. General Wolfe and our troops would be landed there. Marines, Highlanders and redcoats made up our army. There were Rangers from the American colonies, men who were rumoured to fight as savagely as Indians. Word was that they could barely wait to engage the enemy. Now and again some of our ships opened fire, the great cannons thundering as flames shot from their mouths. The enemy fired back, white puffs of smoke rising from their muskets.

"Do you think we will go ashore to fight?" I asked Tom. Once again he had guided me up into the ship's rigging.

"We are sailors, and sailors fight on a ship. Leave the land battles to the redcoats and the others," he said, passing me a spyglass.

Québec was in the distance, less than 4 miles from where we lay at anchor. Through my spyglass I could see that the city was composed of a walled upper section and lower section. With its spires and large buildings, the upper part of the town was certainly the finer. It was also much larger. There were a few French ships in the water below it, but nothing that could challenge us. On the other hand, all along the shoreline were camps with hundreds of their soldiers and militia. There were also batteries of cannons. The French had been busy.

But so had we. During the next few weeks, *Pembroke*'s boats helped carry soldiers to Île d'Orléans, where General Wolfe had decided to set up his first camp. Then we helped bring ashore the guns and carriages they rode upon. These were not like ships' cannons, really, but short, stout siege mortars. They fired 13-inch shells that each weighed 200 pounds.

* * *

"How can we ever take the city? It is on the side of a cliff," I muttered one night in my hammock. We had been at anchor for weeks. As I spoke, I scratched King Louis's chin. The dog no longer hid himself now that Ben was gone.

"The mortars will do the job," said Sam. "I hear their shells can fly more than five thousand yards."

"Québec has no hope. And failing that, we starve them out," laughed Baldish. Hunger was not a problem here. Supplies were brought on board every few days. We received fresh beef, pork, beer and bread, so not a man among us was ever hungry. "The first time their stomachs rumble they will surrender," he added.

"And remember that they cannot get their supply ships up the river," Tom said. "When some of our ships are anchored upriver from the town, they will not be able to get anything down from Montréal either."

"They'll have to walk," Baldish snorted.

Time would tell, I supposed, as I shut my eyes. I dreamed of rumbling, or at least I imagined it was a dream, until someone screamed, "All hands! All hands on deck!" The rumbling was the pounding of men's feet as they rushed to their stations. My feet joined in, but once I was on deck I could barely take another step. I stared in horror at what was coming towards *Pembroke*. It was as though the entire river was on fire, and it was flowing right at us!

"To the boats! Bring lines and grappling hooks!" shouted an officer. All around the ship the same orders were being given. We struggled to launch the boats and arm ourselves to do battle with these monstrous things.

"Curse the French and their fire ships," Tom grumbled. "Now we must go out and tow the wretched things. Can a man get no rest here?"

Five of the fire ships floated past us, sparks rising into the wind and threatening to catch our warships on fire. There were dozens of other small boats in the water besides mine, all trying to defeat the

French attack by capturing the fire ships and towing them to shore. The smoke stung my eyes and I could feel the tremendous heat from the flames that rose up into the sky. It was a hellish scene.

We had to get as close as we could to the fire ships before we tossed grapnels to snare them. With the wind and powerful current, I did not know if I could do my part. Standing in the bow of the boat with a grapnel in my hands, I felt the weight of responsibility upon my shoulders. If I missed and the fire ships reached our warships, men might burn to death.

It all brought to mind that fire back in Halifax, the night I'd saved Baldish. But by some miracle, I did not miss. How far I had come since that night.

One or two of us suffered burns and singes, but not a single one of our ships was damaged. We later agreed that the French had made a mess of it. Though fire ships could be deadly, the enemy had set these ones on fire too soon. The burning hulks had either sunk or had been towed to shore.

"We did it! I cannot believe we were so lucky," I said afterwards. Ben and his fate popped unwelcome into my mind. He had been an unpleasant fellow, but to be shot and killed . . . no one deserved that.

"A man born to be drowned will never burn to death," said Gum cheerfully.

"We *will* be lucky if we can get a few hours' sleep," said Baldish with a great yawn. "Things will be busy tomorrow, now that the French have shown their hand."

Before I slept, though, I thought back on the day and wrote about its events in my journal.

I am not one for daily prayer and such things, but I believe it was a miracle that saved us tonight. Mr. Cook said it was excellent seamanship, plain and simple, but I am certain a miracle was involved.

Chapter 7
July 4, 1759

Baldish was right. It was indeed busy for the next days. There were battles on the shore. Muskets popped and spat and the warm air filled with white smoke. Captain Wheelock ordered us to take out all three of our boats and assist in landing more troops. That done, we landed artillery at a spot called Pointe Lévis, where the army's main encampment would be. Our army's camps quickly became like towns themselves. The enemy fired at us, and our warships fired back, cannonball after cannonball hurtling towards the French encampments, trenches and the town. White smoke drifted through the air, as did the distant cries of wounded men and the cheers of sailors when one of their cannonballs struck home and a wall crumbled. We Pembrokes cheered the loudest of all!

There was one British encampment on the south shore at Lévis, another on the north shore on the other side of a small river that emptied into the St. Lawrence as a waterfall. Montmorency, they called it. Tents stood in rows, with cook fires burning. Laundry hung here and there. Most surprising to me was the number of women. It seemed that the army could not get along very well without women.

We and several other ships sailed upriver and anchored at the west end of Île d'Orléans. General Wolfe's army began to bombard Québec in earnest. Our soldiers heated the cannonballs until they were red hot. Only then were they loaded into the cannons. We watched as flames rose into the sky and smoke poured from the buildings. There was little danger to us, even when the French fired back. If their bombs came too close, our ships' defence was to raise anchors and position themselves a bit farther away.

Once, when our ships set a small French vessel on fire, some of us were ordered into one of *Pembroke*'s flat-bottomed boats. Our mission was to tow the French vessel clear of the fleet. There were no men on board, which was a mercy, for the flames were creeping into its rigging and black smoke billowed about the deck.

"Away you go, Jenkins," ordered Tom, "for you are the most limber of us."

Up I scrambled onto the vessel's bow, where I secured a stout line. I stood there a moment as flames licked at the ship, and prayed that I would never experience such a thing on *Pembroke*. What a terrible death it would be. Then I leapt back down, missing our boat entirely and landing in the river with a great splash. When I popped to the surface, everyone was doubled over in laughter.

"No time to look for mermaids," someone shouted, while another man made kissing noises.

I didn't mind. The water had cooled me, and straining at the oars as we towed the French boat safely away was not so unpleasant. We left the French vessel behind when she ran aground, and left our line behind as well. A piece of rope was worth no one's life.

Life continued aboard *Pembroke*. We were like a floating city. There were our warships and the transports, but there were also the ships' smaller vessels. Longboats went here and there carrying troops and equipment. Boats rowed out at night to take more soundings very close to Québec. Mr. Cook was among them. I missed out on that excitement, but others did not. The French were fond of firing down from their upper town, even if they couldn't see what was there.

Now and again a flag of truce would come from the French or from us. It made no sense to me, since this was a war. Officers, though, saw it differently, and so they had to have their polite conversations.

The summer days were hot and steamy, but not as hot as life in Québec must have been, with the city suffering from our endless bombing. On and on it went for weeks. And although the French returned our cannon blasts, it was clear from the fires that raged through the city that the damage we were causing was immense. One afternoon in late July, word spread that Québec's cathedral had burned. This caused a great cheer to rise up from the crew, since most of the sailors distrusted the Catholics.

On the last day of July, a great battle took place at the Montmorency waterfall not far from the city. A few days before, word had come that we had taken Fort Niagara. Perhaps this would be another victory, I thought, as we watched from up in the rigging, for *Pembroke* was among a number of ships that were supporting the army.

Then the transport carrying the soldiers ran aground some distance from the beach! Our smaller boats began taking hundreds of our soldiers ashore.

"British Grenadiers," Tom told us, gazing at the shore through a spyglass. "And Royal American troops. You will see some hot fighting now, my lads."

"They had best get to it," said Gum, gazing at the dark clouds that grumbled above us. "There is weather coming."

We passed the glass back and forth as we watched the soldiers leaping from the boats and wading in. Once there, instead of marching in their usual rows, the grenadiers began to rush at the cliff. The cannons of our ship *Centurion* gave support to them, booming out like thunder, but the French had the advantage. They could pick our men off easily. My heart sank as they fired down from their positions at the top of the cliff, a cliff that was impossible for our troops to climb. Our soldiers fell by the dozens, red coats becoming redder with their own blood. They must retreat, I thought, before every one of them is dead.

It was then that we were struck by a tremendous storm. Back down to the deck we scrambled. Lightning zigzagged across the black clouds and rain came down sideways. Wind whipped around me, shrieking through *Pembroke*'s rigging. There was no more sound of cannon fire, though. Both sides' powder was completely wet. Later we learned that almost 450 of our brave soldiers had been killed or wounded.

* * *

"General Wolfe's officers dislike him," Davy told us as we were repairing one of the sails a few days later. Now and again squirrels would swim over from the shore and chew holes in the canvas. They were worse than rats!

"How would you know such a thing?" I asked him.

"I heard some marines talking," he said. "His own officers think that we never should have attacked the French near the waterfall. General Wolfe has fallen into disfavour."

Perhaps that is why the general turned his attention to the farms and towns along the river in August. The soldiers and some of the sailors were ordered to burn everything, and burn they did. Not a day passed without black smoke rolling into the sky. When the wind was right, we could smell the stink of it. *Pembroke*'s flat-bottomed boat was ordered out to help with the task. Our mess counted itself lucky that we remained with the ship.

"Not a job for sailors," said Gum, shaking his head. "No honour in it at all."

"They say that there will not be a farmhouse or barn left standing when this is done," Tom told us at supper. "As for the cattle and such, what they cannot drive along with them, they slaughter and leave to rot."

"I hear the Rangers are doing their worst," said Baldish with a small shudder. "Or maybe their best."

"What do you mean?" asked Davy, putting down his spoon.

"Scalping," said Tom.

"But General Wolfe has ordered the men not to scalp," said Davy. His hand went up to rub his head.

"Unless the man is an Indian or a Canadian dressed like an Indian," I explained. "If that is so, the Rangers may scalp as many as they wish."

"I do not think it will improve the humour of our enemy," said Baldish gloomily. "It is enough to make a man wish he had never come."

"For once you are right, Baldish," said Sam in a low voice. "It is enough to make a man think twice about all this. It's not worth dying for."

Sam's words were gone from my mind as I stood watch that night. All during supper, rumours had circled like flies around rotten meat, rumours about what had happened after Fort Niagara's surrender. A good number of Canadian men, women, children and French soldiers were sent down to New York. But others were not so lucky.

Those were given to the Iroquois, who demanded a large number of captives and scalps.

The thought made my neck prickle, and every sound seem dangerous. The river was quiet, but I could still hear it rushing along *Pembroke*'s sides. Now and again water droplets plopped into the St. Lawrence. *Plop, plop, plop,* and then there came a louder plop and a splash. When I looked over the side, I could see that someone was in the water. I drew in breath to shout out an alarm. That is when Blue Sam turned and looked up at me. It was only for a second, and then he was gone. Had he fallen? I doubted it. His look had told me otherwise. He *had* thought twice and was willing to desert and take his chances. As for me, I was still the king's servant, but I had no intention of passing judgement on Blue Sam.

"Man overboard!" I shouted. "Blue Sam is in the water!"

They found no one. Captain Wheelock questioned me sharply, but I remained fast. Blue Sam had gone overboard. Whether it had been an accident or intentional, I could not say. We recalled Sam saying that he could swim, but here the current was strong. Finally Mr. Cook wrote in the log, *Departed this life, 25th of August, 1759, Blue Sam Taylor.*

The next morning Sam's possessions were sold to those who had coin to pay for them. Mr. Cook then sent what was left of our mess ashore to cut wood. Cramming our feet into shoes — how the dratted things pinched after months of not wearing them — we boarded the boat to go ashore. Since he was feeling poorly, Gum remained behind and another fellow named Ed Parr was ordered to take his place.

Once we reached shore, Tom remained behind with the boat, a musket cradled in his arms. His eyes skittered around. Davy, equally armed, followed the rest of us into the forest, where he would stand lookout while we worked. I took my spyglass from my pocket and slowly scanned the water for canoes. Seeing none, I set the glass down on a stump and picked up my axe. Best not to think about what might be creeping around in the shadows. Best to just work, which is what we did, sweat dripping down our faces and bodies. Finally Tom ordered an end to it. Evening was coming.

"I would say we have enough. Another stick," he added as we walked back to the boat, "and one of us will have to swim home."

"My father's glass!" I said suddenly. "I left it back there." In my mind's eye I could see it standing on the stump.

"*You'll* be the swimmer, then, Jenkins, if you do not hurry," teased Ed.

I hurried, hearing Ed's good-natured grumbling about sailors who left things behind. I was not quite able to ignore the spot between my shoulder blades which might draw an arrow as surely as a magnet draws iron. It was then that I heard Ed scream.

I ran, all thoughts of the glass gone from my head. Not into the woods, but back to the edge of the forest, unable to do anything else, running towards the sound of musket fire, the howling of the Indians, the shouting to "Row, row!" and Ed's horrible shrieks.

He was crawling across the sand, gore streaming down his face, the top of his head an open wound. A shrieking warrior held poor Ed's scalp in his bloody fist, waving it about triumphantly, droplets of blood spattering into the sand. Beyond the terrible scene was the boat, the men pulling furiously away from shore. I was stranded.

"Run, William!" cried Baldish. "Run or the savages will roast you alive!"

I ran. Away from the sound of Ed's skull being clubbed into pulp, away from our salvation in the boat. Away from the thudding of the moccasined feet that were now pursuing me. I ran until the breath burned in my lungs and nearly split my side. Still I ran, branches whipping across my face. A musket fired. I felt nothing at first, and then pain bloomed across my calf as blood began to soak my stocking. I staggered, tripped, fell. The image of Ed's smashed head leapt into my mind. Then my own hair was in someone's grasp, my head jerked back. I felt cold metal, and a flash of hot bloody pain.

"Akwi!"

It was an Indian, but *not* an Indian, speaking urgently. A Canadian, I thought through a haze of fear so sharp it stank. Militia. Was he pleading for my life? If so, I wished him all the luck in the world. I could feel my eyes bulging with terror as one of the Indians threatened me with his tomahawk. I held my hands up to protect myself.

"Get up," the Canadian said in passable English. "Get up before I change my mind and leave you to them, *sauvage.*"

"Give him to the Abenaki," said another of the Canadians carelessly. "They deserve trophies, as pitiful as this one is."

"Non, mon ami," said the first Canadian. His face was beginning to swim about as my vision blurred. "This one we take to the officers. A little poking. A little prodding. Perhaps a hot coal

applied to particularly sensitive parts. He will talk."

"Are you a deserter?" asked the other Canadian. "If so, you may tell us what you know, and things will go easier for you."

Ben's words rose up in my mind. *If you are ever taken, do anything you can to survive.* But then I remembered what Mr. Cook had said. *Without honour, life is meaningless.* I did not know which of them was absolutely right. I only knew what I had to say.

"I am not a deserter, sir. I am a loyal servant of King George. Long live the King!" Then I vomited mightily at my captor's feet.

One of them tied a filthy scarf around my leg, and they pushed me through the woods. The branches of saplings whipped against my face and legs. Then we were in a small clearing on a beach where a party of Indians waited. I knew these must be the Abenaki. They stared at me coldly while the Canadians spoke to them in their own tongue. My own eyes remained on the ground. Insects buzzed around us, as bloodthirsty as the men who had captured me.

"We will wait until dawn before taking you in," said one of the Canadians. "Try not to die before then, loyal Englishman."

That is what I did. I sat there in the dirt, my calf throbbing as the night slowly passed. I prayed that rescue would arrive, even though I knew it would not. It would be madness to send men into the forest at night.

* * *

I slept, but it was long in coming, for I wondered if I might be murdered. The Abenaki's faces had been filled with cold threat. Crickets and night insects sang in the woods, but all I could hear were Ed's horrible howls when they'd scalped him. Would that same fate be mine?

Finally, when the sun was just coming up, I was ordered to my feet, and we made our way to the beach. Three canoes had been hidden in the bushes. The Abenaki carried them down to the water and launched them. I was motioned to get in. I could see lamps still burning on *Pembroke* and some of the other ships. Did they think I was dead? Was anyone mourning me? Were my few belongings — and my journal — being sold at the mast right now?

The canoes slid almost silently over the water, driven by the steady paddling of the Abenaki. *Pembroke* was quickly left behind as we drew closer and closer to what was left of Québec's lower town. When we drew into a small harbour, the light was bright enough for me to see just how much damage we had done. Not a building was left intact. What had not burned lay in crumbled piles of stone. The whole place smelled of rot and ashes, but most of all it smelled of despair. The streets were filled with rubble, broken furniture, rain-soaked books with their pages all swollen. A child's doll lay on the cobbles, its cloth head torn off, and again all I could think of was poor Ed and his terrible death. A dog wandered by in search of food, its tail between its legs. I know how you feel, I said to myself.

There was a great flash, and then another and another. We all turned, and that was when I heard the thunder of the British cannons and mortars on Pointe Lévis. One of the Canadians swore in French, cursing all things British.

We left the Abenaki behind. I supposed that they were not permitted in the city, and would go back to their own camp. It was a steep climb up the choked streets and then along a passage that led to the upper town. My calf pulsed in time with every step. Blood was seeping from under the cloth and running into my shoe. The climb was also a fearful one, since not for a minute did the bombs stop falling. Thirty-two-pounders were the biggest of them, and if one of those were to hit us we would be blown to pieces. On the other hand, if the artillerymen decided to load the cannons with jagged chunks of iron and pieces of chain, we would be *cut* to pieces. The thought made my stomach clench.

It was then that one of the cannonballs struck the side of a building. Jagged bits of stone flew everywhere. I fell to the ground, my ears ringing, my heart pounding. A Canadian dragged me to my feet, heedless of the blood that was running down his cheek from where a shard of stone had struck him. One of his companions lay motionless in the street. The others picked up the body and on we went. I couldn't help staring at it. That could have been me, I thought grimly. My life over in one second, with one cannonball, just like that.

As we neared the gate, I could see the silhouettes of soldiers on the wall above us. They called down a greeting and one was shouted up by the Canadians. On we walked through streets that were filled with rubble. Every time a cannonball crashed down, we all cringed and turned away from the bits of wood and stone that pelted down on us. The air became filled with dust and smoke that caused my eyes to water and then run. When I coughed and sniffled, one of my captors sniggered. I suppose he thought I was weeping, but I did not care enough to tell him otherwise.

When we stopped, it was at a small redoubt where a few French soldiers stood at guard. Their white coats were foul with grime, and their faces were fixed.

"What do we have here?" asked a deep voice.

Two men stood in the shadows inside the guard-house. One of them, an officer, stepped into the doorway. I would learn in time that although he was French, he commanded the Canadian militia.

"An Englishman, Capitaine Vergor," said one of my captors.

"A British deserter?" asked the captain with interest, his eyes travelling over me. "Welcome to Québec, Monsieur Déserteur."

"I am no deserter, sir. These men captured me."

"Who are you?"

"William Jenkins of *HMS Pembroke*, sir."

On and on he went, questioning me about the ship and her officers, about what role we had played in the fighting, about what were Wolfe's plans.

"The general does not confide in me, sir," I answered honestly. "I am a simple sailor."

"Simple and useless," sighed the captain.

"You say you are William Jenkins?" asked a voice from the shadows.

"Yes. William Jenkins of *HMS Pembroke*, and before that, Halifax," I said boldly.

"Well, well," he answered. I thought I heard a snort as he leaned his head to one side and stroked his chin, as though carefully considering something. Then he seemed to smile. "I will take this worthless captive off your hands, Vergor."

"Why should I allow that? This is a common sailor, not an officer, and only English officers may be given the freedom to roam the city. You know that. Worthless though he is, he might still be of use in ramsoming back one of our own soldiers. "

"He was once a *capitaine* of sorts. I swear on the sandals of St. Gentian, who is the patron saint of all innkeepers."

Capitaine Vergor laughed out loud, bent over and slapped his thighs. When he stopped, he wiped his eyes, and said, "Patron saint of *innkeepers*! How can you keep your sense of humour after all that has happened, my young friend? Well, I commend you." Then his voice grew more serious. "It would not go well for you if this *capitaine of sorts* were to escape. Understand that. And he will work. By the sandals, robe, beard and tonsure of your St. Gentian, he will work. There is rubble to be cleared."

The two bowed to each other, and then the officer walked off. I could hear him chuckling and muttering about St. Gentian as the hobnails on his shoes clicked against the stones.

"Are you here to question me, as well as make false promises of freedom?" I asked my new jailer.

"I am not."

"Then what do you want?"

"I want *you*, William Jenkins." When I had no comment, he went on. "You are to be billeted with a friend of my family until the army decides what to do with you. And you *will* work. I assure you of that. It should be pleasant enough, in spite of the fact that there is no ice house from which to steal ice. We often wondered what became of you."

"What?" was all I could say in response.

"I said there is no ice house at my employer's home. Nor are there raised garden beds filled with plump cabbages. The siege has seen to that. But there is friendship and adventure of a sort . . . if you behave in an honourable manner, Capitaine Rosbif."

Only one person had ever called me by that name. The speaker took a step forward so that light fell upon his face and the whalebone cross he wore around his neck.

I stared at the birthmark on his cheek. "Vairon?" I whispered. The birthmark was not so small any more, but the shape was the same — a fish.

He smiled and gave a smart bow. "The very same."

"How is it that you are here? What of your parents? Father and I wondered whether you had been deported with everyone else at Louisbourg."

Vairon raised his hands for silence. The lace cuffs fell back, and I saw that only the forefinger and thumb remained on his right hand. The fingers of the left were fused together by a disfiguring scar clearly caused by fire. He awkwardly picked up the musket. "All in good time. It is a story better told at a crackling fire than in a prison cell. I must have your word, though."

"Regarding what?"

"That you will not try to escape from Québec, and that your behaviour will be gentlemanly and honourable."

I hesitated. It seemed that it was my duty to escape, and if I could not escape, to cause as much mayhem among the enemy as I could. Mr. Cook's words popped into my mind, as unwanted as a tormenting itch: *Without honour, life is meaningless.*

But if there was a way to make trouble for the French while doing it honourably, it was beyond me.

"I give you my word," I said to Vairon, "for the

sake of our old friendship, and your offer of hospitality. I will conduct myself with honour, and I will not try to escape. But I do this reluctantly. For the gentlemanly part, I must be honest: It is impossible. You know very well that I am not a gentleman."

"How could I forget? Capitaine Rosbif always was a scoundrel."

And so once again it was a good enough beginning.

It was dawn by the time we left the redoubt and walked out into the upper town. Walked is not exactly the correct word to describe how we went along. Vairon walked, but I limped. The townspeople I saw looked weary and thin. Only the children seemed unaffected by the siege. They were as thin as the adults, but unlike them, the children ran about and played, almost as though the greatest army and navy in the world did not crouch at their gates.

Everywhere were the ruins of what once must have been a beautiful town. Windows were shattered, and now their expensive panes of glass lay glittering on the streets. The slate roofs had come crashing down, and many of the buildings' walls now had gaping holes in them.

We finally stopped in front of a large stable.

The stone walls were still standing, and the roof was more or less undamaged. The place smelled of horse and manure, even though not a horse was to be seen. French officers would still have their horses, but almost every other horse would have gone into people's bellies by now. There were a few tables and chairs where soldiers were drinking and talking amongst themselves. At the end of the building was a hearth where a thin man of middle years was cutting up wizened carrots for a pot of soup.

"Monsieur Fidèle, this is William Jenkins," explained Vairon, "an English sailor they say we may take in to help clear rubble."

Monsieur Fidèle gave me a hard look. "I do this only because they will pay me to take you. Otherwise you would continue to cool your heels in that prison of theirs."

Later that evening, Vairon told me his story. "We left Louisbourg as soon as war was declared," he began. "Both my parents are safe and well in Montréal. Monsieur Fidèle's tavern is another matter, though. It was destroyed this July during a night of bombing." He looked down at his mangled hands. I could picture him fighting through the flames, clawing his way through burning timbers, shouting out for help. "They say I should thank

94

God that He spared me. Too bad my hands could not have been spared as well. I am in the militia, but all but useless in battle. So goes life, eh?"

"I am sorry," I said helplessly.

"As am I for the passing of your father. You and he were once our friends. I have not forgotten that."

"Neither have I," I said truthfully. "Even though at the moment I am your prisoner." We both laughed at that.

Chapter 8
August 28, 1759

It was a strange sort of captivity, but better than being enslaved by the Abenaki. My wound healed cleanly. The ball had passed right through without touching the bone, though the leg was still sore enough to leave me with a considerable limp — especially as each day I pushed a wooden wheelbarrow from behind the stable out onto the street where Fidèle's house had once stood. I swept up glass and shovelled up rubble. With my bare hands I loaded the wheelbarrow with chunks of stone and broken pieces of slate. Privately, I believed this to be an entire waste of time. What was the point in cleaning up the damage when each night the British cannonballs only caused more. But it seemed to give Fidèle some satisfaction. "I must clean it up," he would shout from the door of the stable. He intended to rebuild his home once the British had gone. At night when I lay in the hayloft where we made our beds, I sometimes wondered if the war had not driven Monsieur Fidèle just a little mad.

If it was madness, it did not stop him from thinking up endless errands for us. The man never stopped needing something. Tobacco, brandy, sausage — all things Vairon purchased from soldiers. He also made purchases from the servants of wealthy people, goods that I strongly suspected had been stolen. These things he sold to various customers, which explained in part why he was so popular. Vairon's favourite source of goods was Governor General Vaudreuil.

"He will not miss any of it, and if he does, that is his problem. Vaudreuil is a worse scoundrel than Capitaine Rosbif, you know," Vairon told me.

"Is that possible?"

"Definitely. He and our swine of an intendant, Bigot, have been looting Canada for years. All the goods that come to Québec have always gone into the hands of Bigot or Vaudreuil, and the prices they charge for goods would make a stone weep."

"Far worse than Rosbif, I would say."

We would walk here and there, Vairon with his musket cradled in his arms. Although he could barely fire it now, it was too much a part of him to leave behind. It was on one of these errands that we came upon a crowd lined up on either side of the street. Everyone was cheering, old men were weeping with joy, and women were holding up their babies to see the amazing sight — at least, I assumed it was amazing from the way everyone was acting. And now, I suppose it was, although at that moment I only saw a line of French soldiers marching behind a man on a horse.

"It is General Montcalm," Vairon explained. "He has a house here in the lower town where he lived for a while. These days he is almost always at his headquarters at Beauport. Perhaps he has come into Québec for a council of war."

What I saw was a man of middle years with a white wig upon his head, and a tricorne upon the wig. He had the look of an aristocrat, although he did wave and smile. It was a weary smile. What the people saw was clearly a saviour. The cheering rose and rose as the crowd followed along behind him.

"They say he has been in the army since he was a boy," said Vairon.

"They say the same thing about General Wolfe," I told him as I watched the general move away. What if Wolfe and Montcalm had met as boys the way Vairon and I had? Would it have made any difference now, I wondered. But it was a foolish thing to wonder, and there was ground to cover in our errands. I set the thought aside.

There was also listening to be done, and the best place to do it was right there in Monsieur

Fidèle's stable. The man had tavern keeping in his blood, and so it had not taken long for him to open an establishment in that outbuilding. Like Mrs. Walker, he brewed his own spruce beer. I believe his was even worse than hers, but the men who came here seemed to like it.

The army was on short rations in spite of the fact that supplies had come overland from Montréal. It was the reason many of them bought Fidèle's food, which was a thin eel soup. To avoid being shot by the enemy, Vairon went out at night during low tide to check the weir he had constructed of twisted branches. He had placed the woven fish trap down at a cove they called L'Anse au Foulon. When the tide was low, he could easily check the trap and bring back eels for the tavern's pot.

However, I believe the real reason that men came to the tavern was the entertainment. Monsieur Fidèle, as it turned out, was not only a tavern keeper, but a musician. His instrument was an odd thing called a hurdy-gurdy, which looked a bit like a guitar but with a fat, rounded body, strings and a crank. Monsieur Fidèle scoffed at this English name.

"Hurdy-gurdy. My instrument should properly be called a *vielle à roue*, which means wheel fiddle," he said.

"Why?" I asked him. "Hurdy-gurdy is what the English call it."

Vairon made a rude noise. "Because hurdy-gurdy is an insult to a beautiful instrument, as well as to us. I've been told that hurdy-gurdy has something to do with wriggling your rear end. Perhaps not, but it makes for a good story."

The air of Fidèle's tavern would turn bluish as the men smoked their clay pipes and listened to the whining music. More importantly, the clients grew more and more loose-tongued. I listened to all the conversations and slowly pieced together as much as I could. Bougainville, Montcalm's assistant, continued to patrol the north shore of the river upstream of the city. Governor General Vaudreuil and General Montcalm despised each other, and everyone despised Intendant Bigot. As for the British, Wolfe had all but abandoned his camp at Montmorency in early September. His army had burned all the houses there and off he went. Now he had taken up a position on Pointe Lévis. So had most of the British ships. Although the French had done their best to blow them out of the water, the ships had managed to sail up past Québec.

* * *

"If you ask me," said Vairon as he wiped a table, "it makes no difference where your ships anchor.

We can outlast them. And your General Wolfe is unwell. It seems that he suffers from a fever."

"Not good," I said. It had been raining heavily for several days, making the first week of September miserable. I had been assigned the task of sweeping up the mud the clients tracked in.

"On the other hand, there has been talk of an attack for some time. But then some say that our General Montcalm is also unwell," Vairon went on. "Imagine it. Two generals waving swords about while their *aides-de-camp* hold basins for them to vomit into."

"Not a pleasant picture," I replied slowly.

Vairon must have caught something in my voice. He turned and looked at the doorway. But it was not my tone, it was something else. *Someone* else. There stood a tall man. He gave Monsieur Fidèle a message.

"There is to be a prisoner exchange," Fidèle told Vairon. "The English are returning one of our brave soldiers to us. Take this one to Capitaine Vergor at the new barracks tomorrow. Do you hear me, fool?"

"I hear you, monsieur," Vairon replied.

My eyes were fixed on the tall man. Since he had entered the tavern, his attention had been fixed on me. "Well, shipmate, imagine finding you here," said Blue Sam. He smiled, but it was a smile that was as cold as that of a dead man. "Did you jump *Pembroke*? Or are you a spy?"

"Hello, shipmate," I said quietly. "No spy or deserter. Simply a prisoner."

It was dark, but I could still read his eyes. There was defiance in them and not a small bit of shame. He had deserted, after all. But what exactly had he deserted? Was he an American sailor, a servant of the king, or an Indian? He had been dragged from one life, thrust into another, and then been pulled unwilling back into the first. Besides, who was I to judge?

"Ah. Well, it could happen to anyone. And now you will go back. What a sweet welcome you will have on *Pembroke*."

"As you would have yourself, Sam. After all, you . . . fell overboard. Accidents can happen to anyone," I said, shrugging my shoulders. "There is no black mark against your name."

How he laughed at that. "Fell overboard, did I? Well, Jenkins, good luck to you. Anyone who would not betray a fellow sailor deserves it. May you survive this war, return to Halifax, and live there until you are a very old man."

I might have said something similar, but I did not. Blue Sam *was* a deserter. If captured by the

British, he would be executed. If he returned to the Abenaki, he would be an outcast in the white world. I did not think he would live to be old at all.

"Fair winds to you, Sam," was all I told him.

It was difficult to sleep that night. All I could think of was returning to *Pembroke* and what a great stroke of luck this prisoner exchange was for me. It had happened a few times during the siege, of course. A flag of truce would go up and the fighting would stop. Officers or their representatives would meet and chat politely to make the arrangements, and then back would go the prisoners to their own sides. Once when an officer was captured and taken to the hospital here, arrangements were made for his own clothing and bedding to be brought up to the city. It was as civilized as that. And as simple.

The next day was the 12th of September, and promised to be as hot and humid as any had been that summer. Just after dawn, Vairon and I left the stable and walked through the quiet streets. We did not speak. It felt as though Québec was holding its breath, just as I was holding mine.

Although I could not see her, I knew that *Pembroke* was out on the water riding at anchor. And soon I would be on her again. If there was a patron saint to thank for that, I was more than willing to thank him or her all my life. So it was with a light step that I passed by the bored sentries and entered the barracks with Vairon. It was with an even lighter step that I followed him down the hallway and into a small room where Capitaine Vergor and a second man stood. Then my feet faltered. For the other man in the room was Boston Ben Fence. Would there be no end to vanished people suddenly appearing!

He had changed a great deal since I'd seen him take an arrow and fall into the water. He must have made it to shore, only to be taken prisoner. The swagger had gone from his shoulders. Now they slumped. His hair was matted and his eyes dull. Whatever had happened to him since the day of his capture had broken him. There was still his anger simmering below the surface, though. That had not changed at all. But he was here, and although he was not a man I liked, I have to say it somehow pleased me.

"Were you too tough to kill?" I asked him. He looked over and gazed at me blankly. "I suppose Boston Ben Fence was more than a match for the Indians," I went on. "It is me, Ben. William Jenkins."

"Jenkins?"

"Yes. Jenkins from *Pembroke*. I am to be exchanged, and I thank my stars."

Capitaine Vergor cleared his throat. "There has been a mistake, Monsieur Fence, as I told you. Whoever brought you here to me did so without my orders. It is this *officer* who is being exchanged today. You will remain here with us."

"Officer! This man is no officer. He is not even an ordinary seaman."

"Of course he is not an officer, Monsieur Fence. Do I look like an idiot? Do you think I was taken in by such a flimsy lie? But he *is* the one your Mr. Cook asked for by name."

"I care nothing for that! I must see my son." Ben turned to me, frantic. "Another fellow from *Pembroke* is here — captured a few days ago. He says that supply ships came in from Boston. My cousin crews on one of those ships, and was trying to find me to let me know that my son took a terrible fall — he lies unconscious back home and nothing anyone does can stir him. The doctor thinks he may never waken. I must talk to my cousin to find out more."

"I am sorry for your trouble," I said, and I meant it.

Ben opened his mouth to say more. I could see it in his eyes, but the words did not come out. Let me go free in your place, he wanted to beg, but he simply could not. Begging was not his style, and so Ben squared his shoulders and stiffened his spine. "Enough said," he snarled. "Take me back to my cell then, and good riddance, Jenkins."

"Mr. Fence must take my place," I said before Ben could leave the room. "I am quite content to bide my time here picking up garbage."

"Your Mr. Cook will not be pleased," said Capitaine Vergor doubtfully. "His message made it very clear that it is *you* who is to be exchanged."

"He will understand. Mr. Cook has also always been clear on the matter of honour. After all, this is the only thing, the honourable thing, to do. And if I *were* an officer I would want my honour to be above question."

Capitaine Vergor looked at me thoughtfully, then shrugged his shoulders. "Very well. You could find yourself in a far worse situation here, however. Our native allies do make demands on us, as you probably have heard. Ah. I see you have."

He must have seen me flinch. How could I not recall the fate of those French prisoners from Fort Niagara who were handed over to the Iroquois because the Iroquois thought it their due? Those prisoners had been slaughtered. "Perhaps I will be luckier," was all I could think of to say.

"Perhaps you will." He turned his attention to Vairon. "I am returning to my post in a few hours.

Boring work, if the truth be told, but then someone must watch that wretched Foulon Road."

I inclined my head to Ben and said, "Give my best to our comrades, shipmate. And I hope you get word that your son has wakened." Then before my nerve was completely gone, I left the room, Vairon behind me.

"You *are* a fool, you know," Vairon said cheerfully as we walked back to the stable.

"I suppose I am."

If Monsieur Fidèle was surprised to see me at his doorstep once again, he did not show it. I suppose that after all he had seen in this war, nothing would ever be a surprise again. So he ordered me to my wheelbarrow, and I spent the rest of that day salvaging articles from what had been his kitchen. A kettle, some spoons made of horn, a brass candlestick, a cracked chamber pot. I had no idea what use he would find for that last treasure.

That night there were few patrons at the stable, and all of those were civilians, since most of the militia was out with Vergor in the woods. Cannon fire sounded continuously as our guns bombarded Québec without mercy. Moths fluttered in and out of the open windows. Now and again one would hurl itself into a candle's flame, and with a small snap was gone. It lowered my spirits even more to see this, and all at once the siege seemed hopeless. Were we the moths flinging ourselves into Québec's flame, or was it Québec that was dashing itself against all of England's burning glory? I fear there was no answer to that question, and so I served beer and wiped tables until the sweat ran into my eyes.

Monsieur Fidèle put away his hurdy-gurdy and went up to bed, saying that he may as well sleep through the invasion.

It was too warm up there to sleep. Vairon agreed, and so the two of us spread out blankets behind the tavern. I fell into a restless sleep in spite of the cannon fire. A while later, it was not cannon blasts that woke me, but the whining of a mosquito. I had become that used to the sound of war.

Around three in the morning, shouting erupted from people running in the streets. The British were coming ashore at Beauport, they cried.

"There is no hope for sleeping," said Vairon. "I think we will go down and check my trap. At least it will be cooler for us by the river."

I could scarcely believe that he had invited me to join him, but he had. I felt the curse of my promise not to escape hanging over me. Leaving the stable's yard, we walked out into the night. It was very still and quite dark, since the new moon cast no light at all. We crossed the entire city and exited through the St. Louis gate. The guards, recognizing Vairon and knowing his errand, waved us through.

After so many days of being within Québec's walls, I felt a wild rush of freedom. It seemed as though the air out here was sweeter and the sound of the crickets more pleasant. For the next hour we followed the Foulon Road, down a long field that stretched between wheat fields and pastures. A few houses, their windows dark, sat peaceful. Although I could not see it, I knew that the St. Lawrence lay some distance to our left at the bottom of the cliff. Finally, an owl called from one of the groves of trees that lay ahead, and another answered. That is when Vairon stopped.

"Capitaine Vergor's camp is just beyond those bushes. He has eighty or so men, militia who are seasoned fighters. Indians, too," he told me. He pointed in the opposite direction. "A path starts over there, about thirty paces away. Since to continue down this road would take you right to Vergor, the path is your only choice. It leads to the beach. You need to be very careful when descending, and you need to be as quiet as possible."

"What path? Why are you telling me this?"

Vairon had turned and was walking towards

camp. He stopped and faced me. "Mostly because if someone were to come upon an Englishman in the dark, I suspect that Englishman would lose his hair and his life. Take care, now."

"I have given my word not to escape."

Vairon sighed and rolled his eyes. "You gave your word to not escape from *Québec*. You may notice that you are no longer *inside* Québec. Enjoy your freedom and practise your French, Capitaine Rosbif. When the French army has helped the Canadians win this war, it will be the only language you need."

I hardly knew what to say. What would this cost Vairon if he was caught releasing me?

"What is your business out here at this hour?" called a voice in the distance.

"It is a matter of eels," Vairon shouted back, and there was great laughter as unseen men welcomed him.

I walked as quickly as I could pick my way forward in the dark. Where there were a few soldiers, there might be others. I felt that unpleasant prickling between my shoulder blades at the very spot where an arrow might hit. It remained with me as I worked my way through the trees, listening, listening, my body damp with sweat. When the trees opened up, I knew I must be near the edge of a cliff. Below me I could hear the St. Lawrence rushing along.

I clutched at tree branches and dug in my heels as I climbed down the steep, narrow path. As I descended, the air grew cooler and the scent of the river began to fill my nostrils. I slipped and slipped again, my shoes skittering on the shale. The branches of trees were the only things that saved me. I could have said something very foul about the route Vairon had sent me upon, but I was making enough noise as it was. I kept the remark to myself and concentrated on not falling.

The path ended at a small cove, the one they called L'Anse au Foulon. Now that I was here, I had no idea what I was going to do. Hide until it was near daylight, then move to the beach and hope that someone on one of our ships might spy me? Try to swim for it? But the current was very powerful.

My thoughts flew back to a small cove near Louisbourg where Vairon had taught me how to swim. If I made it back to *Pembroke* I would be facing him in battle. That was as certain as the coming and going of the tides. Could one friend find the courage to kill another? How much loyalty to a king would that take?

I heard splashing and then silence. Perhaps a

duck had taken off. Perhaps a muskrat had chosen to dive. Perhaps it was a French soldier with his musket pointed at my back or an Abenaki ready to fling a tomahawk.

It was none of these. I knew the shape of what was out there as well as I knew the shape of King Louis's head under my hand. How could I ever mistake one of our navy's flat-bottomed boats? The faint light of the coming dawn glinted dully on the coat buttons and bayonets of the men in them. I could make out the red cloth of their coats as the boats turned and began to head for the cove.

I watched in silence as the eight boats came closer. Other smaller vessels were behind them. Waves lapped against the bows and water splashed as the oars dipped and rose. Officers gave their orders in low voices, the oars were raised, and one by one the boats crunched onto the beach. I raised my hands to show that I carried no weapon, and began to walk towards them.

"Stop where you are or you are a dead man!" an infantryman hissed. The soldiers next to him levelled their muskets at me. I stopped, not wanting to be a dead man at all.

"I am not armed," I told them.

"Come forward," said an officer. He lifted a

handkerchief and coughed into it. "Although what I shall do with another deserter at this point is beyond me."

It was General Wolfe. He wore a plain red uniform coat and breeches, clothing that would not draw attention to himself. A black tricorne sat upon his red hair. Around his left arm was tied a black mourning band. Was it for all our men who had died, I wondered. Or was it for the many more who would be killed this coming day?

"I am not a deserter, sir. I was taken prisoner nearly three weeks ago when a party of us from *Pembroke* were — " But the general was already walking past me, and so I trotted along to keep up. Soldiers began to scramble from the boats. "From *Pembroke*, sir. At least one of us was killed and scalped."

"Curse the scalping," he muttered. Then he said, "Make yourself useful then, sailor. There are soldiers to be brought in, ammunition and gear to be carried, and six-pounders to be dragged up."

"Cannons, sir?"

"How else do you think we fight a battle, my boy? With stockings filled with mud?" He flicked a bit of lint from his immaculate cuff. "No, by my word, it is with the blood and sweat of loyal men. Are you loyal to your sovereign?"

"I am, sir. Very loyal to his majesty."

"I knew it! Now make yourself useful. You will remember this glorious day all your life, lad."

Chapter 9
September 13, 1759

General Wolfe would never know how right he was.

For the next while, the Royal Navy brought the army ashore. It sounds like a simple thing. It was not. First to land were the hundreds of light infantrymen who had accompanied General Wolfe. They were armed with muskets and seventy rounds of ammunition. Each soldier also had two days' rations and canteens filled with water and rum. While more and more troops arrived, twenty-four volunteers and an officer scaled the cliff. They crept upward like insects on a wall, clutching at roots and branches. It was an amazing sight, one that left us sailors shaking our heads at the nerve it must be taking. I kept waiting for someone to come tumbling down and smash on the beach below. But the troops kept climbing.

Until those men had secured the top, the assault could not begin in earnest. I stepped back near one of the boats, to better see their progress, and nearly bumped into one of the oarsmen.

"Watch where you put your big feet," he hissed. When he saw who owned the feet, he whispered, "William! As I live and breathe!" It was Baldish. "Boston Ben said you were in the town. Escaped, did you?"

"Baldish! As *I* live and breathe, it is good to see you! Yes, I . . . managed to get away. But how is *Pembroke*? How are you?"

"Still here, as you see. Less hair than ever. And you have missed a night of adventure, I will tell you that."

Pembroke, he explained, was safely at anchor, being too large to come in close to shore. But it had been some of her crew that had joined in to create the diversion at Beauport.

Baldish laughed. "Old Montcalm thought the whole army was there. We can cause quite a disturbance when we put our minds to it. As you well know."

"That I do."

We heard gunfire and saw flashes from the barrels of muskets at the top of the cliff. War cries and whooping came next. Cannons boomed out from a nearby French battery in an attempt to sink and destroy our vessels. The cries of wounded men could soon be heard, but even that did not stop the boats from coming in and offloading more infantry. And it did not stop the army from taking the battery, either. Once that happened, the French guns were silent and our ships safe.

I made myself useful, as I said I would, carrying powder, shot and supplies from the boats. The soldiers continued to come ashore, a river of red that now flowed up the Foulon Road to the heights. They would be having a far easier time of it than the men who had scaled the cliff. And there was also a stream of prisoners coming down, many of them wounded. I was glad to see that Vairon was not among them.

Capitaine Vergor, though, was. Musket balls had passed through his hand and leg. Unconscious, he moaned as they carried him past. The tide was low now and the current not as speedy, so he and the other wounded were rowed across to where a field hospital had been set up in a church at Pointe Lévis. I joined in this task, taking up an oar and settling myself behind Baldish in one of the flat-bottomed boats. Our miserable passengers delivered, we stood by to receive more orders. Some of the boats would carry even more soldiers across. Ours, though, would ferry something rather different, and deliver it to General Wolfe.

It was one of the six-pounders, a brass field gun complete with its carriage. Under the command of an artillery officer named Captain-Lieutenant Yorke, we wrestled it into the boat, then loaded in the equipment necessary for firing it. What a sight we must have been as we rowed back across the river, that gun riding in our midst.

Once at the beach, we wrestled the heavy piece out of the boat. "Let us thank our stars that it is only this small gun, and not one of *Pembroke*'s," I said, wiping sweat from my brow. "I would not much enjoy carrying Deadly Raker around."

"Tell me how small you think it is once we have it up there," laughed Baldish. "What I would not do for a couple of strong horses right now! Six hundredweight if it is a pound."

The sky darkened as clouds rolled in, and it began to rain. But what was a little rain in light of what was happening? Some of us took up the gun's drag ropes and began to haul it across the beach, Yorke calling out encouragement. Others pushed. There were hundreds of sailors milling around. Not many of them were smiling. Instead they cursed angrily and complained as they parted for us. They wanted to be in on the fighting. Who were these officers to deny them that right? There had been sounds of fighting up there for hours, some grumbled. The battle would be over, and not one sailor would have had a chance to draw blood.

The six-pounder grew heavier with each step I took. The sky was lighter by now, but I barely saw anything for the sweat running into my eyes. None of us spoke except Captain-Lieutenant Yorke. Instead we grunted and gasped as we strained. My arms felt as if they would be torn from my shoulders. Sweat soaked my shirt. Someone near me cursed under his breath. It was like dragging *Pembroke* herself.

But every hill has a top and so did this one. There at last, we hauled the weapon through the woods. I could hear muskets firing. Had the battle begun without us? We pulled the field piece along the road until we came out on the high plain where the battalions were already forming up at the spot General Wolfe had chosen. White smoke hung in the air.

"Where are the French?" I wondered aloud.

"Hiding in their town," said Baldish. He cupped a hand behind his ear. "I can hear their knees knocking."

He was wrong. There may not have been soldiers present, but woods to the north of our troops were filled with Indians and militia, who were firing on our soldiers. Many of our men were stretched out on the ground, since it was safer to reload that way. The rest of the army stood motionless, waiting for their orders. There were six blocks of men that I could make out, thousands of soldiers. Grenadiers, regiments of foot, Royal Americans, Highlanders and the light infantry had been formed up in a sort of rectangle, with most of them arranged in two lines with about 35 feet between them. We were ordered to drag the six-pounder close to a hill near the south end of the line. The other gun was already in position at the north end. Our gun was happily received by the artillerymen, some of whom gave us dark looks. They were not as dark as they might have been, since General Wolfe was nearby, but still they made no sense to me.

I raised an eyebrow at Baldish.

"We have touched their precious gun," he said under his breath. "We have dirtied it with our nasty sailors' hands. Well, they shall see what a sailor is made of." And with that he stepped into the ranks of the Louisbourg Grenadiers. Other sailors did the same.

"Thank you, men," the general called out. "Good job. Good job indeed. Now back to the beach with you."

"God bless your honour," shouted Baldish. "Pray let us stay and see fair play between the English and the French."

General Wolfe smiled a little. "I do insist that

you men go. You have done your work. Leave this to the army." And he turned away to deal with the matter of the battle.

Some of the sailors obeyed him, but Baldish worked his way farther in amongst the grenadiers.

"He gave us an order," I said, following his lead. "He is a general, after all. Be sensible, Baldish."

"Sensible? These soldiers should not have all the fighting to themselves. We will come in for a share some way or another."

"Well, perhaps that one has no sense," laughed one of the grenadiers. He was a tall man, as they all were, his height made greater by the mitre hat he wore. "No sense, but enough courage to face this day!"

I could not let myself be seen as a coward, so I joined Baldish. On the other hand, we were lacking certain important equipment. "We have no muskets or cutlasses," I pointed out.

"Give it time," said the grenadier. "Our orders are not to fire until the enemy is forty yards from the points of our bayonets. There will be muskets on the ground for you shortly."

The muskets of dead or wounded men, was what he meant. I was turning *that* over in my head when French soldiers in their white uniforms began to appear on the hillside. They formed up in ranks, just as our army had done, while the militia and Indians kept up a ceaseless harassment of the regiments on the far left and right of us. At their head was a man on a horse. I knew exactly who it was. Montcalm.

The French drummers began to relay his commands. Out they flowed from the general to his officers and to their men. Led by Montcalm, they began to move. General Wolfe positioned himself on the hill to the right of us. Suddenly the French began to run down the hillside. They raced through the trees. Some leaped over puddles. Others had to climb the fences that stretched here and there.

"Fools," said the grenadier with satisfaction. "Look at them. Montcalm's army is falling apart."

And it seemed to be exactly that which was happening. Instead of neat lines of men, the French were advancing in three ragged groups. None of them was heading directly to our centre! All the while their Indian allies screamed, while the French saluted their king with *Vive le roi! Vive le roi!* We stood very still, and not a weapon was fired. That was not the case with the French, though. They paused more than a hundred yards from us, and began to shoot.

"Idiots," said the grenadier again. "Impossible to hit anyone at that range. And look at them. I wager no order at all has been given to fire."

Still, we waited. And to me these men did not seem like fools at all. What they were was something very dangerous, very deadly. They were not marching in straight lines the way British troops would be, but they were no less a threat for all that.

It was then that a strange thing happened. They stopped and stood their ground some hundred yards away. Musket fire erupted from either side of us as the militia and their allies fought from the trees. Our batteries at Pointe Lévis bombarded the city and the cannons there answered back.

For almost three minutes we all stood motionless, staring at each other. Then the French began to fire, but it was a scattered affair that seemed to have little effect. Two of our regiments began to advance and all two thousand men seemed to fire at once. With General Wolfe leading them, the grenadiers did the same, and so Baldish and I went with them. Soon I could not see Wolfe at all, since clouds of white smoke had begun to fill the air.

Nothing I had experienced on *Pembroke* had prepared me for this. To watch a battle from the safety of the ship was one thing. To practise with small arms or to fire her guns was another. But to be in the midst of it while men screamed and fell? Blood spattered across my shirt as one man dropped silently to the ground, half of his head gone. I picked up his musket and ammunition.

"Do not think. Just do your duty," I said aloud. I ripped a paper cartridge apart with my teeth, primed and loaded the weapon. Then I fired. I lost count of how many times I did this or whether I hit anyone. I only know that it seemed to go on forever. The six-pounders boomed as their loads of grapeshot tore into the French. Battalion upon battalion fired until it sounded like one endless volley.

Then the infantry charged and I ran with them. The ground shook with the firing of cannons and the pounding of our feet. Some men were screaming out battle cries, others were running with their teeth clenched in silence. Musket balls smashed onto men's bodies and they fell to the ground, shrieking. I should have been afraid of death at that moment, but all I felt was the thrill of what I was doing.

The smoke cleared a little, and I faltered. There was General Wolfe on the ground. Officers leaned over him. So, strangely, did a woman — presumably one of the camp followers who had attached herself to the British army. It seemed that she was willing to face battle. A bloody handkerchief was wound around Wolfe's right wrist and his shirt was soaked through with gore.

"They run! See how they run!" an officer shouted in excitement. It was true. The French army was retreating, and not in an orderly fashion. They ran for their very lives like panicked horses.

"Who runs?" gasped Wolfe.

"The enemy, sir. They give way everywhere."

General Wolfe hissed out an order. The enemy must be stopped from crossing the St. Charles River. He turned on his side, and for a moment I believe that his eyes met mine. "Now, God be praised," he said weakly. "I will die in peace." Then his gaze fixed upon something that no living person could see.

The men who were with him began to weep as they carried his body from the field. I cannot fully explain it, but it was as though part of him stayed behind. The soldiers remained that inspired. Fixing our bayonets, we began to chase the retreating French. Highlanders were charging across the plain, waving their swords over their heads. Some took French prisoners, but others slashed at men as though they were cutting through wheat.

As I watched them, a musket ball tore across the side of my head. Down I went, blood pouring into my eyes. I struggled to my knees. Through a haze of red I saw the Canadians and Indians. Some of them had fled as well, but many were fighting on from the shelter of the trees on the hill. Was Vairon there? The Highlanders, unable to drive their enemy from the bush, began to fall back. The battlefield with its terrible sounds began to fade and grow quiet. So this is what it is like to die, I thought, and then I did not think any more at all.

* * *

I felt someone take off my shoes, and then dig around in my pockets. My eyes popped open as I clapped a hand on the thief's wrist.

He screamed and dropped my shoes. "Beg pardon. I believed you to be dead."

"I am not."

"Gave me a start, you did!"

"I would like to give you more than that."

But it was an idle threat, and besides, he was already moving on to a real corpse. I sat up, my head spinning, and pulled on my shoes. There were bodies everywhere, some moving, some still. The site reeked of blood, smoke and all the things that come out of a man when he dies. Looters were stripping the French dead of anything valuable. Weapons, belts, even the crosses many wore around their necks, were going into the pockets of these dogs. It was a sight that made me sick.

"A scratch only, although you will carry a scar all your life." A woman of middle years peered closely at my face. I had seen her only a short while ago. "You are not a soldier. Must be one of the mad sailors who insisted upon getting into the ranks. What ship are you with?"

"*Pembroke*," I said. Then, "You were with General Wolfe when he was wounded, madam."

"Mrs. Job, if you please. And yes, I was with him," she said. Her voice was all business. "For all the good I could do. In all my years marching with this army I have not seen such a sad day as this. What a loss for us all. You, though, may be patched up. Down to the beach so that you may be taken across to Lévis."

"Where is he, madam?" I asked her.

"General Wolfe? On *Lowestoft*. Where I will attend to him." When I looked at her blankly she said in a more gentle way, "His remains must be embalmed. He will be going home to England." With a sharp nod she bustled away.

I followed slowly. Not everyone was behaving as dishonourably as the looters. Some men had more honour. These fellows were helping to evacuate the wounded of both sides, using handbarrows. The victims moaned in pain as the barrows bumped

127

them along. As for the dead, it seemed they would remain where they had fallen, at least for now. Unbelievably, some soldiers were eating their dinner in the midst of all this!

I was passed by groups of sailors who were bringing up shovels, picks, saws and axes to where they were already clearing the brush from the hills. Of course, I thought as I approached a group of perhaps fifty soldiers, the siege will begin again, and this time it will be here at the city's very gates.

"Have an eye!" shouted an officer. "We are about to execute this scum."

The firing squad stood in a row, seven men whose faces were like stone. The crowd was equally grim, with none of the laughing and chatter that sometimes accompanied an execution. Seven muskets were already levelled at the condemned man. And that man was Blue Sam.

"Ahoy!" Sam called out, and I realized he was speaking to me.

Dozens of eyes turned on me in suspicion. If the condemned man was a deserter, perhaps I was as well.

"No need for another court martial. This lad fought next to me a few hours ago." It was the friendly grenadier. "A braver and more loyal tar you will find nowhere."

"You know the condemned?" the officer asked me. "Have you anything to say on his behalf?"

What could I say? Sam *was* a turncoat, and in fighting against us had committed treason. Under the king's law he must die, but he had been a fellow Pembroke. He had defended me against Ben's bullying.

"Blue Sam was once my shipmate," I said loudly. "He chose to sail a different course than the rest of the Pembrokes." King's law or no, I paused and felt pity rush over me. "He was an excellent topman. The best."

Sam lifted his chin and stared out at the blue sky. The wind rose a little and his long hair lifted. For a moment he looked as he once had when up in the rigging. The pride of *Pembroke*. The officer raised a handkerchief he held in his hand. The dropping of it would be the signal to fire.

"Fair winds, Jenkins," Sam said.

Unwilling to watch, I turned and walked away. Seven shots rang out. I couldn't block out the thud as Sam's body hit the ground.

It was with the heaviest of hearts that I walked to the Foulon beach, where I found Baldish among the wounded. Mercifully, he was unconscious. A tourniquet was tied around his left leg, whose calf was shattered and torn. Even if Mrs. Job or one of the surgeons could save his life, he would surely lose the leg. As I joined the men who were being ferried over to the shore at Pointe Lévis, I fell into luck. One of the longboats belonged to *Pembroke*. And so instead of being taken to the hospital, I was rowed to our ship.

A lump formed in my throat as I watched her draw nearer. Back I went to that day at Halifax when the ferry had taken me across the harbour. It seemed so long ago. But when I was once again on her deck, with King Louis barking like mad as he wound around my legs, the only thing I felt was happiness.

"You are alive!" Tom Pike cried over and over again in wonder.

Davy slapped me across the shoulder every time Tom said it. "Ben Fence said it was so, but we could scarce believe him. Alive!"

"Not for long, if you keep beating him like that," said Gum. "Come, lad. First we shall clean up that wound and then we shall take you to the captain. Later we will find you a bit of bread and cheese for your supper."

"And a clean shirt," said Davy, "for yours is quite bloody."

Captain Wheelock was below in the great cabin. Next to him stood Mr. Cook, his hands behind his back. Both were as serious as I had ever seen them, their faces set in the most Royal Navy manner. I was asked to give an account of my experiences, and so I did, recounting my capture, Vairon, my release. I even mentioned our old motto — *To friendship and adventure.* All of it, right up to the long battle and my part in it . . . the charge . . . the dying men . . .

"Long? Well, a battle can seem to go on without end. Fifteen minutes or so," said Captain Wheelock.

"Which fifteen minutes, sir?" I asked.

"My boy, that is how long we are told it all lasted. There was the skirmishing before and the mop up after, but the battle itself? A mere quarter hour," the captain told me.

"You may close your mouth, Jenkins," said Mr. Cook.

"Yes, sir."

"Good enough, Jenkins," finished the captain. "Return to your mess."

"And take this with you." Mr. Cook held out my journal. "Your possessions were all sold at the mast, of course. I bought this knowing that Mr. Bushell back in Halifax would want to read and perhaps publish it."

"Mr. Cook believes you have the makings of something more than a seaman, Jenkins," said

Captain Wheelock. "If you ever have the opportunity to take advantage of that possibility, do not miss it."

"I will not, sir!"

That night I climbed into my hammock in borrowed clothing, which would do until I could make some of my own. It was, in fact, clothing given to me by Boston Ben. He said not a word while doing so, but Tom and Gum nodded in approval.

"We five are all that is left of the old mess," said Tom, ruffling Davy's hair.

"Six, if Baldish manages to live through his wounds."

The journal I placed under the rolled blanket I used as a pillow. King Louis, his belly bulging with a rat supper, grumbled at my feet. I did not suppose I would sleep. Far too much had happened. I closed my eyes to rest them, and when they opened, it was to the sound of holystones scraping on the deck.

By nine the next morning, all the longboats in the fleet were landing artillery. Cannons, howitzers, mortars were all dragged up the Foulon Road to the plains. It took hundreds of us to haul these heavy weapons, something we did in the naval style. Midshipmen from a number of ships marched along with us. When a cannon or mortar would roll too far to the left, they would shout, "Starboard, starboard, my brave boys." That would help us to haul more to the right. It was something that passing soldiers seemed to find very amusing.

Up on the plains, the French were now firing shells and shot from Québec's walls down onto our army. I heard that several of our army's officers had been wounded. General Townsend, who was now in charge, issued orders regarding the siege. Men were fashioning log walls behind which they would fire, or digging trenches and piling earth for the same purpose.

We heard that General Montcalm had been shot on the field of battle during the French retreat. He had died sometime after that and had been buried in the town. As for us, close to 600 had been wounded, and 61 were reported dead. Those bodies must be buried, and buried quickly. Already they were swelling in the heat, drawing clouds of flies and flocks of crows. It was, I supposed, better than doing what the men out in the countryside were doing. Detachments of soldiers and sailors were still burning scores of farmhouses along the river.

With handkerchiefs tied over their noses and mouths, the burial parties laid men to rest in unmarked mass graves. If the battle itself had been hard, this was worse. At least when you were fighting, you had a chance. These fellows — French, Canadian and English — would never see home again. I kept my eyes from it as well as I could. Friend or enemy, it would have been too sad to see Vairon among those remains. Besides, he had spirit and he had luck. I hoped he lived.

Chapter 10
September 14, 1759

For five days after the battle, we Pembrokes joined in the siege work. Each night we returned to the ship. More and more firing came from the French batteries.

Finally, one morning we all squinted at the signal flags that were being hoisted on *Stirling Castle*. "Signal for a lieutenant," I mouthed silently. One by one the ships launched boats and over went the required officers. Back they came bearing messages.

"Make ready to sail," Captain Wheelock ordered. We all rushed to our positions.

Seven of our biggest ships — *Pembroke* among them — weighed anchor. It was slow, hard labour, as always.

I had watched our warships from the walls of Québec. They were fearful in what they could do. The French would understand that if we came in once again on the night tide, they would be attacked by sea and land.

"They will be reconsidering their stubbornness

now," laughed Tom later, as we prepared to spend the night. He was feeding King Louis a bit of salt pork. "See there! Admiral Saunders is going ashore and the French will give up. If I am wrong about it, may this dog have my dinner for a month."

When dawn broke the next morning, I knew Tom was correct, and so his rations were safe from Louis. There it was: a flag of truce flying over the town. Later, Captain Palliser from *Shrewsbury* came on board and gave Captain Wheelock the news.

Mr. Cook passed it to us. "Québec has surrendered. God save the King!"

How we cheered at this news. I joined the Pembrokes in shouting out "Huzzah!" until my throat was raw. An extra ration of rum was issued for all hands, which was downed quickly. Not having the head for such drink, I traded mine for a clean shirt.

Our task would be to take possession of the lower part of town that afternoon at three-thirty, we were told. The army would do the same in the upper town, raising the Union flag. And so, led by Captain Palliser, a large group of sailors and lower-ranking officers loaded into ships' boats. Each of us was armed. I carried a wickedly sharp axe and prayed I would not hack off my own toes before we landed. Cannon fire that surely was the French boomed out from the direction of the St. Charles River. I wondered if they had not heard that the siege was over.

But there was no resistance. In the cool wind and rain, Québec's citizens were unsmiling, except for some young women who winked at us prettily. Davy made vomiting noises, Tom winked back, but I ignored them.

"They say some of our soldiers and sailors have married girls from this town," said Ben. "Orders have been given forbidding anyone else to do so." That caused Davy to make even louder vomiting noises, which made us all laugh.

We marched up the shattered, rubble-filled streets to a hill overlooking the lower town. There, where all the ships out in the basin could see it, the British colours were raised. It was a splendid moment, at least for us.

Someone whispered that it was four o'clock, and that we should celebrate this day and hour all our lives. The great guns from our ships of war roared out a salute. There were even more huzzahs than earlier, cheers that barely drowned out the sound of the cannon blasts.

"What would General Wolfe think of all this?" I asked no one.

"Not much," Ben shouted back, and I knew he would never change. "For he's dead, ain't he? After all this carrying on, he's dead. His corpse is on *Royal William* now, they say."

"But he *did* it. He won the day. Maybe his ghost is huzzahing with us," Davy suggested. "That would be a fine thing, would it not, William?"

"*We* won the day, Davy," I answered. "He lost all the rest of his. But, yes. It would be very fine, indeed."

That evening I wrote in my journal for the first time in three weeks. The pencil felt a bit strange in my fingers, and my writing looked equally odd. Still, I felt I must put it down.

I cheered when Québec surrendered. Now a melancholy feeling has begun to creep over me. Mr. Bushell talked about how the Romans and Greeks used to march triumphantly into a place when they had conquered it. I am loyal to our cause, but I did not feel very triumphant, I have to say. Mr. Cook says that the terms given to the French were generous and fair. The army will be deported, as will certain prisoners. The citizens must swear an oath to King George, but they may practise their religion, farm their land and conduct themselves as before.

How will they do that, I wonder. How can any of us? It has all been at a very great cost, I fear, and I think that the peace here will be a restless one for a long while. Still, when I consider that men on both sides were willing to pay that price . . .

I was not certain how to end the sentence, and I considered crossing it out. But then, I wrote the only thing I could.

Huzzah, General Wolfe. Huzzah, General Montcalm.

* * *

If anyone thought that winning the battle would see an end to hard work, he was mistaken. Twenty-five English prisoners were brought on board, all of them deserters. They would be tried and executed back in England, for there was seldom any mercy regarding desertion. We continued to land supplies and bring down French artillery from the upper town. There was the daunting task of bringing on board the ship's two twenty-four-pound guns that had been at Lévis all these weeks. And almost 700 pounds of fresh beef were loaded onto *Pembroke*, while we watched four transports set sail for France. On them was the French garrison. It all amounted to several good days' employment.

On the 23rd of September our mess was given a day of shore leave, and it was with great excitement that we put on clean clothing, braided one another's hair, and made ready to explore Québec. All except me. I had seen enough of Québec. Still, I wanted to see Vairon. Surely he and Monsieur Fidèle still lived.

"Come on, William," said Tom. "All work and no play makes for a dull tar."

"Dull as old paint," added Gum. "And you know the town. You may give us a tour."

"Let Ben show you," I said. "He has been there as well."

"But, William," said Davy, "Ben did not see where General Wolfe fell. I must see it myself if I am to tell my grandchildren the glorious tale some day."

It seemed like a good idea. Now, though, I wonder what Davy will tell his grandchildren. We saw nothing of glory. Instead, the setting of Wolfe's death was melancholy. Even with the dead buried, crows still haunted the field. And the city itself was a shell of a place. The bishop's house, the cathedral, the convent — all were in ruins. Hundreds of houses had burned and those that remained had huge holes that you could see right through. The streets were filled with more rubble than ever, and pocked with enormous craters. That did not stop bands of soldiers from looting, though.

Davy's spirits dropped lower and lower. Mine did no better.

Finally Tom said, "I suppose there would not be a tavern left in this forsaken mess? That would be too much to ask."

"Perhaps there is," I answered.

And so it was that we came to be standing in front of Monsieur Fidèle's stable. The door was closed and so were the shutters. I knocked. Nothing. I pounded. Still nothing.

"What is that awful sound?" asked Davy.

It was Monsieur Fidèle's hurdy-gurdy, which he was slowly playing as he sat behind the stable.

"Have you come to gloat?" he spat. "If you have, go somewhere else and do it. I have taken the oath of allegiance to your king, just as required. May St. Gentian and *Le Bon Dieu* forgive me."

"No gloating. We have merely come for your spruce beer," I told him. "And I hoped for a bit of news of Vairon."

Fidèle said nothing. He simply led us inside, the hurdy-gurdy cradled in his arms like a baby. Once the beer had been poured into cups, he sat down heavily and said, "Vairon is dead."

"No," I said, as if that could stop it from being true. A dull ache spread through my stomach. "You are . . . certain?"

Monsieur Fidèle nodded. "I did not see the body myself, but others did, and there was no doubt it was him, what with that bone cross around the corpse's neck. And I cannot tell you just where his grave is. So many were placed there together, you know." Monsieur Fidèle gave a great sigh. "Vairon was a good fellow, but not a very convincing liar. He always told me how tasty my beer was. We all know otherwise."

My heart heavy, I hoisted my cup and said, "To Vairon. He was a true friend, and a brave man."

It had been a terrible day. And yet even a terrible day can have a bit of brightness. We discovered it when we went across to Pointe Lévis, where we found a pale, thin Baldish in a field hospital tent. But he was alive, and the sight of him smiling at us was a great relief.

"They took my leg from the knee down, as you can see," Baldish said. None of us except Davy cared to look too closely.

"You must miss your leg terribly, Baldish," said Davy.

"Not too badly," said Baldish.

"But now you cannot be a topman," said Davy, and Baldish just laughed.

"However, he can and likely *will* be a cook," explained Tom. "It is a fine position often given to wounded men. And better work for a one-legged man cannot be found anywhere."

Back on board *Pembroke*, rumours were swirling. It was only a matter of time before the fleet left here. We, like all the other ships, had given up all of our ammunition and powder to the army. It would be their job to hold Québec now that our part was all but done. We would be bound for England, Boston or Halifax, depending on the whim of Admiral Saunders. And Mr. Cook had left *Pembroke*! Admiral Saunders had appointed him master on Lord Colville's ship *Northumberland*. Mr. Cook's star seemed to be rising.

"Boston," said Ben that night. He was quite cheerful, since he had received word that his son had regained consciousness. "I hear we New Englanders will be homeward bound by the end of the month. Even if it is just talk, it warms my heart. What a thing it will be to see my boy again."

Ben once told me that if you want to understand just how much you are missed when you are gone, put your hand in a bucket of water. Then take it out. That is how much of a hole you leave.

But Mr. Cook *has* left a great hole. I wish I had been able to say farewell and thank you. The new master, Mr. Cleader, is not half so interesting.

But I gave it no more thought. For the next

few days, as the end of the month crept closer, we Pembrokes made endless trips from the ships to Foulon. Every bit of gear and food that could be spared was going to the army. It would be a long, hard winter here, and I did not envy those who had to live through it. At least those monotonous trips kept me from thinking. My thoughts would not have been the most cheerful.

Chapter 11
October 1, 1759

That first day of October, Ben Fence and the other remaining Yankees were ordered to go aboard a transport that was bound for Boston. I believe it was the first time that I ever saw Ben truly happy. He had never been a popular man, but he was our messmate, and so we gathered together to bid him farewell on deck. One by one he shook Davy's, Tom's and Gum's hands. Then he came to me. Although my own hand was extended he did not reach out to clasp it, which I suppose should not have been a surprise. But then he stepped forward and gave me a great hug. Now that *was* a surprise.

"I owe you a debt, Jenkins," he said. "If not for you . . ." He could not finish.

"If not for William you might have stayed at Québec and married one of those French ladies?" suggested Davy. And we all — even Ben — roared with laughter.

Boston Ben Fence was gone. Within two weeks, we were readying to do the same. *Porcupine* and *Racehorse* remained anchored in the basin. They would spend the winter here to help support the army. The rest of us prepared to sail down the river. Some ships were destined for England. *Pembroke*, though, would return to Halifax. Under the command of Lord Colville, she and four other battleships, three frigates and a number of sloops would winter there.

"This should be simple," I said to Baldish. "We will be going downstream after all." Baldish was back on *Pembroke*, limping around the ship assisted by a rough crutch. As Tom had predicted, he was now a cook's mate, and as happy as a pig in muck.

"Nothing is ever as simple as it should be," said Baldish.

He was correct. Our voyage began nicely enough. There had been a heavy frost the night before, but the day was fine. As we weighed anchor, Admiral Saunders's ship saluted the garrison with twenty-one guns. The garrison returned the gesture. Hundreds of people — civilians and military — lined the walls of the upper town and the wharves of the lower to view the spectacle. All ships' flags were flying at half-mast in honour of General Wolfe. His embalmed remains now rested in a coffin aboard *Royal William*. He was indeed going home. My thoughts flicked briefly to Vairon, and then I set his memory aside. There was no time for sadness. There was only time for tending to the ship.

It soon became clear that for all our soundings and setting of buoys, the river was still tricky. We may have conquered Québec, but we certainly had not conquered the St. Lawrence. The currents near Coudre Island were treacherous. Several ships ran aground, including *Royal William*. Someone made a joke about how General Wolfe would like that, seeing how seasick he had become in the past. All the laughter sounded hollow to me, though. Another vessel, *Terrible,* had to lash a cannon to two of her small anchors to avoid being swept away. How her crew sweated and strained. We were luckier, and so managed to get past safely.

During the next days we slid down the river. All up and down the shore the trees had changed from green to red and orange. Those trees were the only pleasant things to be seen. Almost all the farmhouses and outbuildings were in ruins. Once I saw a small boy standing by the shore. He made a very rude gesture, and then ran away. I cannot say that I blamed him.

When we finally reached the gulf, the ships parted. Our squadron changed course and continued to Halifax. The rest of the ships set out for England.

I was up in the rigging taking in the view. I watched for a long while as the ships grew smaller and smaller and then finally became white specks on the horizon.

By the 27th of October, Halifax was in sight. It amazed me that the granite lighthouse on Sambro Island was almost completed. What a difference that would make for any vessel. In the distance I could see Mather's Meeting House as well as the governor's mansion. There was the church and the stockade. And above it all stood the Citadel, still on guard. All along the shore were people waving and calling out. It was as fine a greeting as anyone could want.

"Is it good to see Halifax?" asked Tom.

"Yes, my friend," I replied. "Good indeed."

He laughed. "And it will be even better to walk its streets. Some of us will be spending the winter ashore, as you know. But there is a bit of work to do before that. Until then, none of us will have shore leave." He grinned at me. "Although I hear that you will be leaving us early next month, Jenkins. Imagine, you will be done with a life at sea!"

Tom's "bit" of work turned out to be a monstrous amount. *Pembroke* and the other vessels all had to be readied for winter, which is what we did for the next while. Under the direction of the new master and the bosun, we took down the enormous sails and folded them. The sailmaker and his men would spend the winter doing repairs to the canvas. The yards and upper masts were lowered to the deck. So was all the running rigging that raised, lowered and controlled the sails. We coiled it all into enormous bundles and carried it below with the canvas. Then there was the messy task of greasing the rigging so that it would not rot during the cold weather. That, of course, was assigned to me and a number of other unlucky fellows. We caulked shut the gun ports to keep as much cold air out as possible. Small stoves were brought aboard. We made them as secure as we could. No one wanted to have the ship go up in flames.

When one of our boats had gone ashore I was able to send a note, telling Mr. Bushell I was well. I was to be discharged on November 3rd, and perhaps we could meet at Mrs. Walker's. Other than that, I could only gaze at the town. There I saw some of the smallest vessels, the one-masted sloops, having the bottoms of their hulls cleaned. This was done at the partially finished naval yard where a careening dock had been built for that very purpose. When the tide went out, I could see the vessel settle to the sand and lean over against the dock. Then sailors scraped away the seaweed and barnacles that always grew on the under part of the hull. When the tide came in, away the boat sailed. It was an amazing sight.

Then, late on the morning of November 3rd, Mr. Wise told me that my service on *Pembroke* was over. That evening he struck my name from the ship's muster book by writing a large *D* next to it. That meant discharged. I could see many other men's names that had *DD* next to them. Discharged dead. He gave me my pay — 40 shillings — and that was that.

With King Louis under my arm, and my few possessions in a seabag, I left our mess for the last time and stepped onto the deck. Out in the distance the transport ship *Mary* slowly drifted around her anchor. Aboard were more than 150 Acadians who had been hiding in the woods. They were bound for England at any moment. Poor wretches, I thought, and my memory flicked again to Vairon.

"Do not forget us," said Davy.

"With that empty head of his, it will be quite a challenge," laughed Baldish, saluting me with his crutch.

"We will see you at Mrs. Walker's once this slavery is ended," said Gum.

"Then we'd best step lively," said Tom. "Look at

the gulls. See how high they fly? I fear there may be weather."

The harbour, though, was quiet and the sky a dull pewter colour. The boat slid along through the water with only the oars rippling its surface. Not a breath of wind stirred. I looked back and waved, but my messmates had gone below.

Once ashore, I walked down Water Street feeling rather low. King Louis raced ahead with not a care in the world. That, as well as the weight and sound of coins in my pocket, lifted my spirits. Halifax had not changed, and yet it had. The mud was the same. So were the rough plank buildings. The Great Pontac Inn was as grand as ever and so was the governor's mansion. Hardened men still stood in doorways while horses pulled wagons laden with barrels or stacks of goods. Dogs trailed behind them, or chased cats between people's legs. I could see that King Louis wanted very much to join in. He had not seen another dog or cat in a very long while. But naval discipline won out, and he controlled himself.

When I arrived at Mrs. Walker's, she hugged me until I nearly choked. Word was sent to Mr. Bushell that I was there. Since it was a Saturday evening, the shop was closed and he soon arrived. It was the jolliest reunion you could imagine, with complete strangers joining in. Even Mrs. Walker's spruce beer seemed to taste excellent.

"Read to us from your journal, my boy," said Mr. Bushell. As I did, the room grew quiet. All eyes widened as the tale of my adventure slowly filled the room.

I was only an hour into the story when I heard something. We all heard it. A low roaring had begun.

Out we ran. A massive storm was racing towards Halifax, black clouds boiling behind a white squall line. When it hit, every boat and ship began to swing into the wind and strain at its anchor. The ensigns and pennants streamed straight out and snapped madly. Men were racing around the decks, making things fast. Several small vessels that were under sail heeled over violently when the wind hit them, and one capsized. Then sheets of rain began to drive down, and the harbour disappeared. So did we, taking shelter inside. And as the storm grew more violent, it was clear that we all would be spending the night.

"Plenty of rooms," said Mrs. Walker. "And I will give them to you free of charge!"

Even with the amazing price, I barely slept. The inn shook with each blast of wind — wind that howled like a hundred wolves. King Louis shook as well, and he was a seasoned sea dog! When dawn came, the storm still raged on. We made the best of it, though, for there was nothing else to do. Mrs. Walker cooked and chattered about news in the town. The men played cards and dice. It was almost as though I had gone back in time, but somehow it did not feel right. And I could only imagine what was happening aboard *Pembroke*.

Another restless night passed, and another bleak morning. Then, as suddenly as it had begun, the great storm was over. The sun came out and a fine rainbow appeared. People began to creep out of their houses, blinking like owls. And there was much to blink at. Boats lay on the beach, their sides stove in. Many of the wharves had collapsed, pounded to bits by the storm surge. Much of the flour and sugar in the warehouses was ruined, which caused the women to shake their heads.

"No sweet desserts," mourned Mrs. Walker.

"It did not seem to bother the navy, though," said Mr. Bushell.

It was true. The navy ships rode calmly in the harbour, just as though nothing had happened. His shop was another matter. Water had flooded the floor, and half the wooden shingles on the roof were gone. At least the precious printing press had been spared.

During the next days, I helped Mr. Bushell with repairs to his roof while I decided what to do with my life. But with every nail I pounded, I grew more and more discontented. I do believe I miss having a deck under my feet, I thought to myself.

"Jenkins, you look out of place here," Mr. Cook called up to me. He had just bought a newspaper. "You are more suited to rigging than a roof."

"I suppose I am, sir," I answered as I climbed down the ladder.

"See here. I supped with Captain Wheelock on *Pembroke* last night," Mr. Cook told me. "This package came for you when dispatches arrived."

"Thank you, sir."

"Jenkins," he went on, "*Northumberland* is as short-handed as the rest of the ships — there is always room for another midshipman."

"Me? A midshipman?"

"You will be rated a captain's servant in the beginning. The only serving you will do is to your books, though. I will instruct you in navigation. If you study hard and prove yourself to Lord Colville, a midshipman you will be."

"Yes, sir. I will study hard, sir."

"Report to *Northumberland* when your work is finished here. And bring this fine little dog of yours. Excellent ratter . . . in spite of the hairs."

"Yes, sir. Dog it is."

As Mr. Cook walked away, I opened the package. Inside was a letter written in French. And there with it was my father's spyglass! As I translated the note, my smile grew and grew.

My dear Capitaine Rosbif,

I am writing this at my parents' table in Montréal. Rather than submit to you English, it seemed wiser to leave Québec. I regret there was no time for a proper farewell. And I regret even more that you believed I was dead. That I learned when Monsieur Fidèle wrote to my parents and told them the sad news. I was very pleased to write back to him and tell him he was wrong.

As for your spyglass, it was in the hands of one of Capitaine Vergor's scoundrels, who had gotten it from an Abenaki. I traded my bone cross for it. That man was killed in the battle. You understand now why that unlucky fellow was mistaken for me.

So. Montréal will surely fall next spring. I will not be here to see it, though. Tomorrow I depart for the west. They say there are enormous bears in the mountains, and herds of buffalo that blacken the plains. No Englishmen, though. Perhaps you might like to see these amazing things for yourself some day. Until then, I remain your servant, Vairon.

"What was that old motto of yours?" Mr. Cook called over his shoulder.

"To friendship and adventure!" I shouted back. And I heard him laughing as he headed up the street.

"Vairon is alive," I said happily to myself. Then looking down at the dog, I added, "Well, King Louis, I suppose I must sharpen my pencil. There will be many more chapters to add to my story before it is done."

Epilogue

That winter, William rejoined the Royal Navy, enlisting on *Northumberland*. His future was once more linked with Mr. Cook's. In the spring of 1760, when the French threatened to retake Québec, a squadron of British ships including *Northumberland* returned to the city to support the British troops. The effort was a success and so Québec remained in British hands.

Back in Halifax that fall, he watched Mr. Cook as the master worked on charts of Halifax harbour. Cook could see how keen William was regarding map-making and surveying. For the next few summers William often accompanied Cook as he set out in a ship's boat to explore and chart the Nova Scotia coastline.

But in 1762, the French attempted to take Newfoundland. It was an important fishing base. *Northumberland* joined a squadron of British ships that sailed to St. John's, where the French fleet was anchored. When fog and a gale enabled the French ships to flee, the British easily retook the garrison. There would be the lengthy process of negotiating a treaty, but for all purposes the Seven Years War was over. *Northumberland* sailed for England that October, and William left his world in Halifax behind.

For the next few years William continued to live a life of adventure. He returned with Mr. Cook to Newfoundland when Cook was ordered to survey the coast. Each winter they sailed back to England, where Cook worked on his charts and William studied.

William was promoted to master's mate. He accompanied Lieutenant Cook — he too had been promoted — on two of his voyages to the Pacific. On the first, in 1768, they sailed on HM Bark *Endeavour*. William and the others saw New Zealand, Australia, New Guinea and Java. Through panes of smoked glass, they also observed a rare event, the Transit of Venus, as that planet made its stately progress across the face of the sun.

On the second voyage, in 1772, Captain Cook — once again promoted — circumnavigated the globe, taking HMS *Resolution* across the Antarctic Circle three times, and sailing farther south than anyone had ever done. It was on this voyage that William fell from the rigging in a terrible storm. When he woke four days later, his left leg had been amputated below the knee by the ship's surgeon.

Resolution arrived back at Spithead, England, in July 1775. William, at age thirty-one, chose to be pensioned off and leave the navy. That summer he considered his options. England was no longer home, and Halifax held nothing for him, what with Mrs. Walker and Mr. Bushell being some years dead. Each of them, however, had left him with a gift of money. With that and his savings — William had been ever frugal — he decided to return to a place he had loved.

That fall, a ship landed at St. John's, Newfoundland. There William met and married Sarah O'Brien, an Irish housemaid. The next summer saw the couple arrive in the outport of Bonavista, where he worked as a clerk at Mockbeggar Plantation, a fishing premises. He and Sarah began to raise a family.

One evening in the fall of 1781, William was drinking in the company of sailors in a local pub. One of them was reading a tattered copy of a British newspaper, *The London Gazette.*

"See here," said the man. "It says that Captain Cook, the great explorer, is dead. Wonder what he did to get himself in such a mess?"

It was true. James Cook had been killed in the Hawaiian Islands two years before, and his body buried at sea. William, deeply moved at the news, but angered by the sailor's words, abandoned his ale and walked home. The walking calmed him. He didn't need to wonder what had happened. He only recalled the best advice Captain Cook had given him, words that had formed the backbone of his own life: Without honour, life was meaningless.

William Jenkins is buried somewhere in Bonavista, Newfoundland.

Historical Note

The Seven Years War

In North America, the Seven Years War was referred to as the French and Indian War, named for those forces the British were fighting. Although the war was also waged in Europe, India and the Caribbean, in North America the battle was for Canada. The Siege of Quebec during the summer of 1759 marked a turning point in fighting that had been long and brutal. Although the war officially extended from 1756 through 1763, the parties had been effectively at war since 1754. The pivotal battle at the Plains of Abraham is most familiar to modern readers. Early in the morning of September 13, 1759, General James Wolfe's army moved upstream in the Royal Navy's vessels. Scaling the cliff below the Plains of Abraham was a bold manoeuvre, one that General Montcalm never expected. That meant there was no real opposition.

Montcalm need not have met the British challenge at all, but that was the nature of war in those days. When his army did march from their camp to the east, they came at a run, and quickly became disorganized. The battle was brief and deadly. It lasted around fifteen minutes, although it must have seemed much longer to those involved. Six hundred British troops were wounded and sixty-one killed. One British officer estimated as many as fifteen hundred French casualties.

Scholars have long debated the wisdom of Montcalm's coming out to meet Wolfe. So have re-enactors and writers. The result of the siege was a tide-turning event.

Some may say that battles are won by armies and their generals. That may be so, and yet the Royal Navy played a very important role during the siege. As this story shows, it provided transportation, as well as all the food and ammunition. It was sailors who dragged the massive guns up to the plains, and then insisted on fighting alongside soldiers. The navy was never really given credit for what it did that summer. But without its support, Quebec likely could not have been taken.

The fleet had gradually assembled at Louisbourg in the spring of 1759. There were 320 vessels, including 49 warships. It faced a journey of 1100 kilometres (600 nautical miles) to Quebec, one that was complicated by ice, fog and the treacherous waters of the St. Lawrence. But seventeen

French pilots — men who knew the river very well — had been captured at Louisbourg the year before. And there were the charts that James Cook had drawn. Organized into three squadrons, the fleet was able to navigate up the St. Lawrence with little difficulty.

According to *Pembroke*'s log, she seems to have spent most of the summer anchored some distance from Quebec. She was too large a vessel to safely sail in waters so filled with shoals and mud flats, and subject to tides. There were other ships nearer the city, though. Three bomb vessels — *Baltimore*, *Racehorse* and *Pelican* — armed with mortars, bombarded the town.

It was important to get as many ships as possible upriver of Quebec. It would put them in a much safer position and allow the British to land troops. In doing so on the night of August 18, though, a vessel named *Diana* ran aground. For twelve hours she was fired upon by the French. It was necessary to throw most of her cannons overboard to lighten her. When she finally floated again, she was sent back to Halifax.

But the fleet did serve well. It was flat boats, longboats, barges and cutters, manned by sailors, that brought the army ashore for the Battle of the Plains of Abraham. Sailors moved ammunition, and evacuated the wounded. The navy provided all the rum and biscuit that the soldiers consumed. Without it, the siege would have been impossible.

HMS *Northumberland* remained at Halifax that winter. On April 22, 1760, *Northumberland* and the fleet set sail for Quebec. On board were new copies of Cook's maps, which had been printed in England. Within a month, the ship was anchored in front of the city.

Quebec had suffered that winter. Many sailors still had scurvy, that terrible condition caused by a lack of Vitamin C. The French attempted to retake Quebec, but by summer's end it remained in British hands. Montreal had surrendered to British troops. *Northumberland* returned to Halifax that fall.

Mr. Cook often took out one of the ship's boats. He produced maps of Halifax harbour and parts of the Nova Scotia coast. Then, in July of 1762, word came that the French were sending a force to Newfoundland to destroy the British fishery there. By September 13, *Northumberland* and the rest of the squadron were at St. John's. A gale rose up, and the French ships were driven out to sea. The French garrison surrendered a few days later. *Northumberland* and the squadron sailed for England that October. Once there, the ship's company was paid off and disbanded. James Cook, though, was not destined for a life ashore.

The war finally ended in 1763 with the signing of the Treaty of Paris. The French would keep St. Pierre and Miquelon, two small islands off the coast of Newfoundland. Accurate charts of those islands, as well as the areas around Newfoundland where the French would still be allowed to fish, were needed. Cook was assigned as marine surveyor during the summers of 1763 to 1767, tasked with mapping much of the coast of Newfoundland. Some years later, Cook would chart Nootka Sound in British Columbia.

James Cook would go on to lead three expeditions to the south Pacific. These resulted in promotions to lieutenant and then captain. He circumnavigated the globe twice and drew detailed charts of Australia, New Zealand and numerous Pacific islands. In 1776 he was admitted to the Royal Society — an organization that promoted scientific research — for so successfully having prevented scurvy in his crew. Three years later, Cook and four marines were killed at Kealakekua Bay in Hawaii. His remains were buried at sea there.

In the age of sail, ships were made of wood, iron and canvas. Salt water, wind and battle took their toll, as did the passage of time. HMS *Pembroke* was no exception. After years of service during war, she was converted to be used as a hulk or storage ship in 1776. *Pembroke* broke up off the east coast of Canada in 1793.

The stories of Cook, Wolfe, Montcalm and all the other historical characters in this book are well known. But there are also the less celebrated folk to remember. There were farmers, common soldiers, sailors and Native allies. Their names may not be known, but they served an equally important part in fighting for what they believed. Like James Cook surveying the shores and rivers of this country, they helped chart Canada's destiny.

On-board Ship

The Royal Navy was made up of many boys. They ranged from boys of six to young teens. Larger ships had a schoolmaster on board for young midshipmen. Boys destined to become ordinary sailors — they were referred to as ship's boys — were trained by sea daddies, such as this book's character, Tom Pike. Whether one was a common sailor or a midshipman, a life at sea could be a good choice of profession. There was steady work and decent food in a time that promised neither. In the future, midshipmen would come from high-ranking families. It would be necessary to have connections and influential family friends. But at the time of this story, a young man without such connections still could be a candidate.

Midshipmen spent their time studying mathematics, navigation and seamanship. They did not wear a uniform at this time, but would have had to supply themselves with suitable clothing. Not only the officers, but seasoned sailors, would be responsible for their training. Midshipmen would be expected to show respect to all of them. It may not have been adventurous, but such skills would be necessary for any midshipman who wanted to be an officer.

Farm animals, cats and dogs could be found on ships of war. The last two helped keep down the population of rats, which could be very destructive. One captain of that time said that his ship was so leaky, he was afraid the rats had chewed through the hull again. There are accounts of parrots and monkeys kept as pets. There are also accounts of tigers, a bear, and even an elephant being carried back to England in the name of science.

Timeline:
The Royal Navy's Role in the Siege of Quebec

May 5, 1759: the fleet of 13 ships leaves Halifax, bound for Quebec

May 15: Captain Simcoe dies

May 17: Simcoe is buried at sea off Anticosti Island in the Gulf of St. Lawrence

May 27: Captain John Wheelock takes command of *Pembroke*

May 28: most of the fleet anchor at Coudre Island

June 8: *Pembroke*, *Devonshire*, *Centurion* and *Squirrel*, along with several transports, continue up the St. Lawrence as an advance party; they take soundings of the river

June 10: a plan of the Traverse has been charted, and the rest of the fleet continue up the river

June 18: *Pembroke* anchors at the east end of the Island of Orleans, upriver from Quebec; *Pembroke*'s boats help ferry soldiers ashore to the island

June 27: *Pembroke* and several other ships anchor at the west end of the Island of Orleans

June 28: the French launch seven fire ships, which the British sailors tow away

July 1: *Pembroke* assists in landing troops at Point Levy

July 18: ships get past the city and into the upper St. Lawrence

July 31: the fleet can see the Battle of Montmorency

September 12 (night): troops begin to land in the cove

September 13: the Battle of the Plains of Abraham

September 18: Quebec surrenders

Several of the thirteen ships from the Royal Navy set sail from Halifax, bound for Quebec, on May 5, 1759.

General James Wolfe (above) was in charge of the British forces on land; Admiral Durell the naval siege. Defending Quebec was French general the Marquis de Montcalm (below).

The French and Canadians sent blazing ships down the river to set the British ships on fire. General Wolfe apparently sent a letter to General Montcalm, stating: If you send any more fire-rafts, they shall be made fast to the two transports in which the Canadian prisoners are confined in order that they may perish by your own base invention.

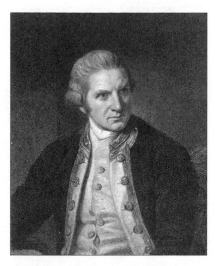

James Cook, ship's master on Pembroke, *charted difficult areas of the St. Lawrence River so that British warships would not run aground en route to Quebec. His logbook entry for September 13, 1759, states in part: "* . . . our batteries at Priest P[t] kept a continual fire against the town all night. At 8 A.M. the Adm[l] made the sig[l] for all the boats man'd and unm'd to go to Point Levi . . . At 10 the English army, commanded by Gen[l] Wolfe, atacked the French, under the command of Gen[l] Montcalm, in the feilds of Aberham behind Quebec, and tottally defeated them . . ." *In ships' logs, short forms took the place of often-used words, such as sig[l] for signal, and spelling was not always consistent.*

British regulars boarded smaller boats to make landfall near Foulon, then sailors hauled cannons up the small road onto the Plains of Abraham, where they would face Montcalm's forces.

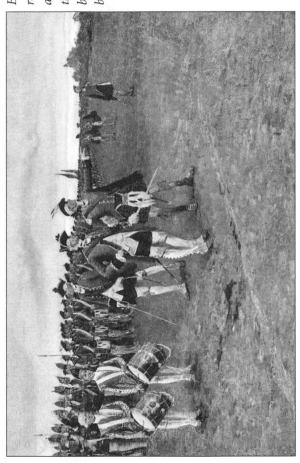

British regulars assemble on the Plains before the battle.

A soldier (left) is shown in the uniform of France's Troupe de la Marine. A private of the 58th Foot (right) wears his traditional uniform.

As shown in this highly romanticized but famous painting, General Wolfe was mortally wounded during the battle on the Plains.

The Royal Navy under sail was an imposing sight. Here, the fleet under Lord Howe sails from Spithead, England, towards the coast of France, in the late 1700s.

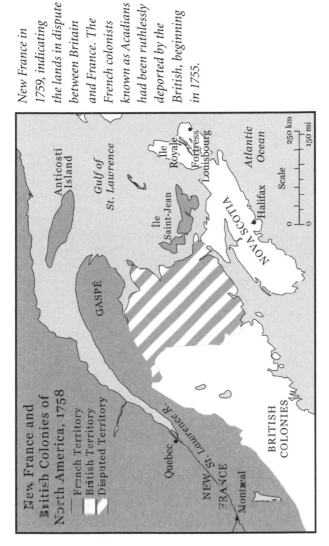

New France in 1759, indicating the lands in dispute between Britain and France. The French colonists known as Acadians had been ruthlessly deported by the British, beginning in 1755.

New France and British Colonies of North America, 1758

French Territory
British Territory
Disputed Territory

Anticosti Island

Gulf of St. Lawrence

Île Royale

Fortress Louisbourg

Atlantic Ocean

Île Saint-Jean

NOVA SCOTIA

Halifax

Scale

0   250 km
0   150 mi

GASPÉ

St. Lawrence R.

Quebec

NEW FRANCE

Montreal

BRITISH COLONIES

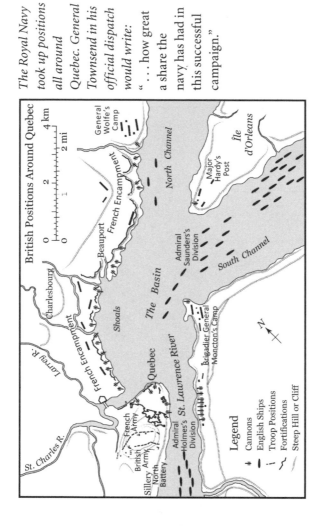

The Royal Navy took up positions all around Quebec. General Townsend in his official dispatch would write: "...how great a share the navy has had in this successful campaign."

British Positions Around Quebec

General Wolfe's Camp

French Encampment

North Channel

Beauport

Major Hardy's Post

île d'Orleans

Charlesbourg

Admiral Saunders's Division

South Channel

French Encampment

Shoals

The Basin

Larrey R.

Quebec

St. Lawrence River

Brigadier General Moncton's Camp

St. Charles R.

French Army

British Army

Sillery

North Battery

Admiral Holmes's Division

N

Legend

Cannons

English Ships

Troop Positions

Fortifications

Steep Hill or Cliff

0   1   2   4 km

0   1   2 mi

Credits

Cover cameo (detail): *Portrait of the Young Ingres (1780-1867)*, Jacques Louis David, Getty Images, BAT:79758587.

Cover scene (detail): *French firerafts attacking the British Fleet off Quebec*, © National Maritime Museum, Greenwich, London, BHC0419.

Page 170: A *View of the Pierced Island, a remarkable Rock in the Gulf of St. Lawrence*, Hervey Smyth (painter), Pierre-Charles Canot (engraver), LAC Acc. No. 1997-2-2, Collections Canada, C-000784.

Page 171 (upper): *James Wolfe*, Joseph Highmore, LAC Acc. No. 1995-134-1, Collections Canada, C-003916.

Page 171 (lower): *Louis-Joseph, Marquis de Montcalm, 1712-1759*, Antoine François Sergent-Marçeau, LAC Acc. No. 1970-188-295, W.H. Coverdale Collection of Canadiana, Collections Canada, C-014342.

Page 172: *The Defeat of the French Fireships attacking the British Fleet at Anchor before Quebec, 28 June[,] 1759*, LAC Acc. No. 1991-19-1, Collections Canada, C-004291.

Page 173: *Captain James Cook*, engraving; copyright © North Wind / North Wind Picture Archives, all rights reserved; PEXP3A-00113.

Page 174: A *View of the Taking of Quebec, Sept. 13, 1759*, LAC Acc. No. R9266-2012, Peter Winkworth Collection of Canadiana, MIKAN no. 3019077.

Page 175: *British army assembling on the Plains of Abraham before taking Quebec, 1759;* hand-colored halftone of a Frederic Remington illustration; copyright © North Wind / North Wind Picture Archives, all rights reserved; EVNT2A-00250.

Page 176 (left and right): *Soldier, Troupe de la Marine, 1759* by E. Leliepvre © Parks Canada; *Private, 58th Foot, 1759* by G.A. Embleton © Parks Canada.

Page 177: *Death of General Wolfe in the battle for Quebec, 1759*, engraving; copyright © North Wind / North Wind Picture Archives, all rights reserved; EVNT3A-00326.

Page 178: *British Navy under Lord Howe sailing from Spithead for battles off the coast of France, late 1700s;* copyright © North Wind / North Wind Picture Archives, all rights reserved; EVRV2A-00081.

Pages 179 and 180: Maps by Paul Heersink/Paperglyphs.

The publisher wishes to thank Janice Weaver for her careful checking of the facts, and Andrew Gallup for sharing his considerable expertise about the Seven Years War.

About the Author

Maxine Trottier's family has been in Canada since the time of the *filles du roi*. Her ancestors were among the founding families of Detroit.

She has a keen interest in history, and has spent many years as part of a French and Indian War re-enactment group called Le Détachement. The group has portrayed Canadian militia and their women at such sites as Fortress Louisbourg, Fort Niagara and Fort Necessity. Maxine says that she feels "very comfortable in the eighteenth century."

For this novel, she found herself fascinated by James Cook's role in the Seven Years War in what is now Canada. Now living in Newfoundland, a place that Cook charted two and a half centuries before, she and her husband often sail the waters that Cook sailed, going in and out of small coves that he named.

In fact, Maxine has always been interested in the sea and its traditions. For two successive summers she spent three weeks crewing on a tall ship, HMS *Tecumseh*. Her duties were very similar to those William Jenkins would have experienced. She says she was "at least as apprehensive climbing up into the rigging," the first time she tried it, "but I did do it." She calls it a thrilling experience, and one she will never forget.

Maxine is the author of three Dear Canada titles: *Alone in an Untamed Land* (shortlisted for the Red Cedar, Red Maple and Silver Birch Awards), *The Death of My Country* (Honour Book, Geoffrey Bilson Award for Historical Fiction) and *Blood Upon Our Land*. Her Circle of Silver trilogy includes a CLA Book of the Year Nominee. *Under a Shooting Star* was a Geoffrey Bilson Award Honour Book, and her picture book *Claire's Gift*, set in Cape Breton, won the Mr. Christie's Book Award. Another picture book, *The Tiny Kite of Eddie Wing*, was a CLA Book of the Year Award winner.

Maxine is also the author of *Terry Fox, A Story of Hope,* and dozens of other books.

* * *

Historical characters mentioned in this book: Governor General Vaudreuil; Captain Louis Vergor; Captain William Gordon of HMS *Devonshire*; Joshua Mauger, merchant; John and Elizabeth Bushell; James Cook, ship's master; Mr. Richard Wise, ship's purser; Second Lieutenant John Robson, Captain John Simcoe; Captain John Wheelock; William Thompson, bosun; Vice Admiral Saunders; Dr. James Jackson, surgeon; Admiral Durell;

Joseph Jones, landsman; General James Wolfe; Dr. George John, surgeon on *Prince of Orange*; Bob Carty, a sailor on *Pembroke*; the Marquis de Montcalm; Intendant Bigot; Captain-Lieutenant Yorke; Mrs. Job; General Townsend, who replaced Wolfe; Mr. John Cleader, who replaced Cook aboard *Pembroke*.

Other books in the
I AM CANADA series

Prisoner of Dieppe
World War II
Hugh Brewster

Blood and Iron
Building the Railway
Paul Yee

Shot at Dawn
World War I
John Wilson

Deadly Voyage
RMS *Titanic*
Hugh Brewster

Behind Enemy Lines
World War II
Carol Matas

A Call to Battle
The War of 1812
Gillian Chan

For more information please see the I AM CANADA
website: www.scholastic.ca/iamcanada